Michelle muttered as she peeked through her sister's living room curtain.

Striding up Brooke and Jared's walkway was none other than Nick Kempner, dressed in black tie and accompanied by his daughter, obviously Michelle's charge for the evening. She adored Kelsey and didn't mind one bit baby-sitting the little girl. However, she did mind the fact that she would have to face the girl's father, especially since he looked like a young version of James Bond with his tanned face contrasting with the tuxedo shirt, his dark hair primed to perfection. At the moment, the doctor was definitely shaking *and* stirring her belly.

Brooke opened the door while Michelle hung back. She moved just far enough that she could still see Nick, but Nick couldn't see her. Enough distance to allow her the opportunity to get a good look at him without him knowing it.

And what a view it was.

Dear Reader,

Escape the winter doldrums by reading six new passionate, powerful and provocative romances from Silhouette Desire!

Start with our MAN OF THE MONTH, *The Playboy Sheikh*, the latest SONS OF THE DESERT love story by bestselling author Alexandra Sellers. Also thrilling is the second title in our yearlong continuity series DYNASTIES: THE CONNELLYS. In *Maternally Yours* by Kathie DeNosky, a pleasure-seeking tycoon falls for a soon-to-be mom.

All you readers who've requested more titles in Cait London's beloved TALLCHIEFS miniseries will delight in her smoldering *Tallchief: The Hunter*. And more great news for our loyal Desire readers—a *brand-new* five-book series featuring THE TEXAS CATTLEMAN'S CLUB, subtitled THE LAST BACHELOR, launches this month. In *The Millionaire's Pregnant Bride* by Dixie Browning, passion erupts between an oil executive and secretary who marry for the sake of her unborn child.

A single-dad surgeon meets his match in *Dr. Desirable*, the second book of Kristi Gold's MARRYING AN M.D. miniseries. And Kate Little's *Tall, Dark & Cranky* is an enchanting contemporary version of *Beauty and the Beast*.

Indulge yourself with all six of these exhilarating love stories from Silhouette Desire!

Enjoy!

Joan Marlow Golan

Joan Marlow Golan
Senior Editor, Silhouette Desire

Please address questions and book requests to:
Silhouette Reader Service
U.S.: 3010 Walden Ave., P.O. Box 1325, Buffalo, NY 14269
Canadian: P.O. Box 609, Fort Erie, Ont. L2A 5X3

Dr. Desirable
KRISTI GOLD

Published by Silhouette Books
America's Publisher of Contemporary Romance

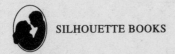 SILHOUETTE BOOKS

ISBN 0-373-76421-9

DR. DESIRABLE

This edition published by arrangement with Harlequin Books S.A.

® and TM are trademarks of Harlequin Books S.A., used under license.
Trademarks indicated with ® are registered in the United States Patent
and Trademark Office, the Canadian Trade Marks Office and in other
countries.

Visit Silhouette at www.eHarlequin.com

Printed in U.S.A.

KRISTI GOLD

began her romance-writing career at the tender age of twelve, when she and her sister spun romantic yarns involving a childhood friend and a popular talk-show host. Since that time, she's given up celebrity heroes for her favorite types of men, doctors and cowboys, as her husband is both. An avid sports fan, she attends football and baseball games in her spare time. She resides on a small ranch in central Texas with her three children and retired neurosurgeon husband, along with various live-stock ranging from Texas longhorn cattle to spoiled yet talented equines. At one time she competed in regional and national Appaloosa horse shows as a nonpro, but she gave up riding for writing and turned the "reins" over to her youngest daughter. She attributes much of her success to her sister, Kim, who encouraged her in her writing, even during the tough times. When she's not in her office writing her current book, she's dreaming about it. Readers may contact Kristi at P.O. Box 11292, Robinson, TX 76116.

To Belinda,
for all those Wednesday-night brainstorming sessions
in a barn apartment, fighting the dust, deadlines
and, at times, insecurity. But most of all,
for being there from the beginning.

One

She had a face designed by angels and a body that could incite a riot.

Unfortunately for Dr. Nick Kempner, Michelle Lewis held him in very low esteem, thanks to that little incident a few months ago at her sister's wedding.

Nick still didn't understand why she had taken such offense at being called a princess. After all, she had looked like royalty in that bridesmaid's dress. And considering she'd called him a toad in a tux, he should be the offended party. Of course, his ex-wife had probably called him worse.

Today Michelle Lewis, in the role of San Antonio Memorial's public relations guru, still looked like a cross between sin and sainthood. She also looked none too pleased to see Nick when he entered the meeting a little late. Okay, so he was more than a little late. Considering Michelle was the only remaining occupant in the hospital conference room, he'd obviously missed the luncheon assembly altogether.

Michelle offered Nick only a cursory glance when he leaned back against the conference table and watched her. She continued to gather her things without so much as a polite "get the hell out of Dodge, Doc."

Feeling like an errant kid, Nick waited for her acknowledgment of his presence. When that failed to come, he gave up and gave in. "So what did I miss?"

"The whole meeting. It ended about five minutes ago."

Nick shrugged. "Sorry I'm late. My nine-o'clock surgery took longer than planned."

Michelle shoved her laptop computer into its case resting on the table. Only then did she give him her full attention. "Since this is the second meeting in a row that you've missed, maybe you should reconsider serving on the committee if it puts a strain on your schedule."

He brought out his best grin. "Maybe we could hold the meetings in the O.R. You could do your presentation while I do a total hip replacement."

The beginnings of a smile curled the corners of her mouth but it didn't form enough to reveal her arresting dimples. "Interesting suggestion. However, most of the physicians manage to work around the monthly meetings without resorting to such drastic measures."

"Well, Ms. Lewis, I guess I'm not like most docs around here. I like to put the patient's needs first. I'm kind of funny that way when it comes to my medical practice." He'd be glad to give her what she needed, anytime, anyplace, even now.

Not a good idea to make that offer, Nick decided, when she folded her arms beneath her breasts and pinned him in place with her intense indigo eyes. "I admit that's an admirable quality, Doctor. But we need all the input from physicians we can get in order to make a successful go of this ad campaign."

Time for a dose of diplomacy. "And how is the campaign going?"

"Very well, thank you. Today we discussed the new pediatric unit's assets and how we'll utilize them in advertisement."

The only assets Nick cared about at the moment were Michelle's. The red sleeveless turtleneck traveled all the way up her slender throat but didn't conceal the outline of her full breasts. The fitted black knit skirt hit her midcalf yet revealed a nice glimpse of leg through the slits up both sides. Her long dark hair gleamed like the polished walnut table behind him, making him itch to test its texture. Those were the kind of assets he could definitely appreciate.

But Nick realized that he wouldn't get anywhere with Michelle Lewis by ogling her, so he pulled his gaze back to her face and his mind back on business. "Exactly what are the ads going to feature? The new pediatric ICU?"

She took out a pair of glasses from the pocket of a jacket draped over a chair and slipped them on, as if that might make her look more qualified. It sure as heck didn't make her look any less enticing. "Actually we're going to spotlight the new family room."

"The family room? Are you sure that makes sense?"

She looked annoyed. Beautiful, but annoyed. "It makes perfect sense. We want parents to know that they have a place to relax when their child is ill. Besides, the majority of people take high-tech equipment for granted. Dr. Rainey pointed that out during the meeting.''

Nick figured Al Rainey was trying to score points with Michelle. Or more than likely just score. That made Nick more than mad. The guy was a class-A jerk, especially when it came to attractive women. Someone needed to remind him that he was married, and often. "No offense, but Al Rainey is a plastic surgeon." And a mediocre one at that. "Face-lifts are his forte, not ad campaigns."

"Actually the idea was mine."

Well, hell, he'd really done it now. "Oh, yeah?"

Michelle frowned. "Yeah. And quite frankly, Dr. Rainey's been very cooperative and insightful. As a matter of fact, he always comes *early* to the meetings."

Nick chose to ignore the dig at his tardiness, but he couldn't disregard her defense of a known hospital lecher. "Rumor has it that Rainey comes early in all his endeavors."

Michelle cleared her throat and blushed like the devil. "Well, he is the chair of the committee and he agrees that we should focus on the family room."

He'd lay money that Al had his focus on Michelle.

Nick couldn't get a handle on his sudden jealousy. He also couldn't resist pushing some of Michelle's buttons, just like she'd pushed some of his at the wedding. Like she was pushing some now. Hot buttons. "I personally believe that if we're going to be taken seriously here at Memorial, we should center on quality health care. That is, *if* my opinion matters, since it takes me a lot longer than Rainey to arrive when it comes to certain undertakings."

Michelle slipped off the glasses and tapped one armature against her chin, looking calm and collected.

But the blush was still apparent on her cheeks. "Of course your opinion is valued, Doctor. And I promise the new equipment will be mentioned in the ad copy. Will *that* satisfy you?"

The only thing that would satisfy him at the moment would be to kiss that sassy look off her face. "Yeah, that pleases me right nice, Ms. Lewis."

Her smile finally made an appearance, revealing her damnable dimples, heralding victory. "I'm so glad you're pleased, *Dr.* Kempner. Anything else I can do for you?"

Oh, yeah, he could think of several things, and none were proper.

Batting the thoughts away like a persistent fly, he gave her a little salute. "Nope, that's all." He answered her smile with one of his own. "For starters."

Of all the confounded cocky doctors, Nick Kempner was at the top of Michelle's list. And a long list it was.

No doubt about it, the man had an uncanny knack for getting her hackles up. It had all started the first day they'd officially met at Brooke and Jared's wedding. Out of respect for her brother-in-law and sister, she'd tolerated him then. Out of respect for her job, she'd tolerated him today. Not that he wasn't really nice to look at.

But she wasn't one to kowtow to men unless absolutely necessary. She imagined that plenty of women would perform back flips for Nick Kempner, or anything else he requested. All he probably had to do was flash his pearly whites and nail them with those mocha-colored eyes and *Whamo!* They were immediately transformed into mindless sheep searching for a slick shepherd.

Not Michelle. She'd had her fill of silver-tongued healers with lovin' on their minds, some sporting a marriage license along with an M.D., as well as a penchant for hiding the truth. Of course, Nick Kempner was unattached. Not that it mattered, considering his reputation with the ladies. Nor did it matter that he was Brooke's husband's best friend, or that Brooke had strongly hinted that Michelle should get to know him better. That was one rocky road Michelle intended to avoid, regardless of her sibling's less-than-subtle matchmaking attempts. And Nick Kempner's overt charisma.

Michelle strode toward the elevators, trailing behind the stream of medical staff returning to their jobs from lunch. At least the meeting had gone well. *After* the meeting was another thing altogether, thanks to Nick Kempner.

"Hey, Ms. Lewis, wait up."

Good Lord, was he following her?

She turned to face the recent burr in her bottom but continued to walk backward. "More concerns, Dr. Kempner?"

"Nope. No more concerns." He gave her a lingering once-over and an optimum grin. A smile designed to liquefy joints. And darned if it didn't.

Feeling as exposed as if she were wearing a half-undone hospital gown, Michelle clutched the computer's case to her chest. "Then what else can I do for you?"

"I just want another minute of your time."

They came to a stop in front of the elevators, and she had to look up at him. She'd reached five-ten during her sophomore year in high school, so looking up at a man wasn't a common occurrence.

"Your ride's here, Michelle," Dr. Rainey called out, his hand battling the insistent elevator doors.

"Go ahead," she said. "I'll catch the next one."

Rainey's smile wasn't nearly as effective as the patent Kempner grin. "Okay. If you're sure."

"I'm sure." She brought her attention back to Nick and impatiently tapped her foot. "Yes?"

"He just beats all now, don't he?" Nick drawled.

"Why, Dr. Kempner, with that accent, one might think your moniker should be Billy Bob."

"Guess my roots are showing."

"Roots?"

"Born-and-bred Texan."

She sent a pointed look at his feet. Cross trainers, not cowhide. Big cross trainers. Big feet. She met his steady gaze. "Oh, those kind of roots."

"Yeah. Not to be mistaken for Rainey's roots. The guy really needs to restock on hair dye."

Michelle tried not to smile but couldn't quite get a grip on her grin. "You really don't like him much, do you?"

"Ah, now, does it show?"

"Just a bit." She leaned back against the wall separating the two elevators, the sudden awkward silence broken only by the operator paging someone on staff. "I really have to get back, so if you can just tell me what you need." Boy, was that leaving herself wide open for all sorts of possibilities.

He zeroed in on her eyes. She wanted to look away, but couldn't. "I owe you an apology for questioning your expertise. And a belated one for my faux pas at Brooke and Jared's wedding."

Apology? She certainly didn't expect that. "Apology accepted, Dr. Kempner. Okay?"

He cocked one shoulder against the wall and faced her. He smelled good, looked even better. "It's Nick, and it's not okay. I got a bit out of hand."

Her reaction to him was getting out of hand. Way out of hand. Her pulse jumped like a cat on a hot grill. She'd been annoyed by his failure to make the meeting on time, and now she was annoyed at herself for finding him attractive. Would she ever learn? "Let's call a truce."

"Good idea. After all, we're in this together."

Now why did that sound so darned intimate? "Yes, I guess you're right."

He pointed at her chest. "Do you need any help with that?"

"Beg pardon?"

"Your computer."

She glanced down. Like a fool, she'd forgotten she had the thing in a choke hold. "I can manage."

Michelle pushed away from the wall, shoved the case's strap over her shoulder and thumbed the elevator's down button. She turned to find him standing not more than a foot away. Really, really close. So close she could run her hand along the ridge of his strong jaw, trace the outline of his lips, the cleft in his chin...

Thankfully the elevator doors sighed open, providing her with a much-needed escape. She backed into the car while Nick Kempner just stood there with hands hidden in the pockets of his starched lab coat, an insolent lock of dark hair falling over his forehead, the V-neck of his blue scrubs revealing a pleasant glimpse of dark chest hair.

He tipped an imaginary hat. "You have a good day now, Ms. Lewis."

Shifting the strap to the other shoulder, she punched

the Open Door button. "Don't you want to go down with me?"

His grin made another appearance, slow as sunrise, and just as bright. "Oh, yeah, that sounds real tempting. But I'm needed up on the med-surg floor for a consult. Maybe later?"

Michelle presumed her face resembled a hothouse tomato. And she'd mistakenly thought her foot was too big to fit in her mouth. Her hand dropped from the button, the doors slowly closed and her last image of Nick Kempner branded her brain—his hand raised in a wave, his smile full of mischief, his dark eyes drilling holes in her well-honed reserve.

Of all the seductive, sexy surgeons, Dr. Nick Kempner was now at the top of Michelle's list. And a small list it was.

The hot August sun beat a large swath across the backyard barbecue, indicating the extreme Texas summer was far from over. A trickle of sweat streamed down Michelle's chest, pooling where the bathing suit top ended below her breasts. She swiped a hand over her forehead, pushing away the damp, rebellious hairs that wouldn't fit into her ponytail. Idiot fringe, her mother called them. Fitting, considering what an idiot she'd been to let Nick Kempner get to her. He was still getting to her, even after two days. Still invading her thoughts, and sometimes her dreams.

She scanned the crowd of partygoers positioned in random groups spread across Jared and Brooke's manicured lawn. Nick wasn't here, as far as she could tell, although she'd been told he was invited. Maybe he was engaged in immoral combat in the pool house with a gullible nurse. That thought annoyingly irritated Michelle.

She sank back in the padded lawn chair and considered returning to the pool. But the pool was now crowded with a stew of kids too thick to stir. Nope, she'd just sit here sipping her lemonade and think about work.

She thought about Nick Kempner instead. Someone should bring her the discarded baseball bat so she could pound him out of her brain. Plenty of docs around to save her from a subdural hematoma.

Her brother-in-law moved forward from one block of people, clutching her sister's hand. Michelle tamped down the wistful feelings when she noted the way Jared looked at Brooke, as if she were goddess of the universe. Brooke used to look at Michelle that way, with sibling adoration, as though big sister Michelle had scattered the stars. Not anymore.

But what could she expect? Brooke had her own life with Jared. Michelle's job and seeing to her parents' needs didn't allow her much time to spend with Brooke. They were both adults now, living adult lives, not giggling kids practically attached at the hip. Brooke didn't really need Michelle as much anymore. As it should be.

Then why did Michelle suddenly feel like a fallen hero?

Jared strolled to the redwood picnic table, hopped onto the bottom bench and let go a loud whistle. "Listen up, folks. We have an announcement to make."

Michelle rose from her seat, securing the beach towel around her waist as she moved forward with the rest of the crowd. Jared sent Brooke another adoring look before turning back to the curious audience.

"As you all know," he began, "I've been on leave since my accident. With the help of my beautiful and talented physical therapist wife, I'm finally ready to go back to surgery."

Applause rang out. Michelle sought Brooke's gaze and gave her a thumbs-up. Brooke responded with a radiant grin before giving her smile back to Jared.

Jared reached behind him and tapped his beer bottle on the table to garner the murmuring masses' attention. "Although that's good news, I've got even better news. During the course of my wife's expert therapy, something else happened."

Holding out his hand to Brooke, Jared helped her up to join him on the bench. They wrapped their arms around each other's waists, forming a cocoon of contentment. Michelle sighed.

"Do you want to tell them, babe?" he asked Brooke.

Brooke nodded, looking more than a little misty. She had a certain glow about her, something Michelle had failed to notice until now. She could almost guess what was about to come, but the thought was unfathomable. Brooke would have told her something so important. Something so life altering.

"We're going to have a baby," Brooke said with a laugh.

Michelle stood stunned as Jared drew Brooke into a lingering kiss. Hurt shot straight through her heart, keen as a butcher knife, twice as painful. Why hadn't Brooke told her first? Why had her sister—the closest person in her life—waited until now to make an announcement that should have been made in private to her family first?

Deep down, Michelle recognized she should be happy for Brooke and Jared. She should be doing back handsprings across the yard and cheering with the rest of the folk, including her mother who was hugging Brooke and crying, and her dad now doling out pats on Jared's back. But she couldn't.

Her fear and hurt wouldn't let her. Hurt because Brooke hadn't told her the news first. Fear for her sister's health: the asthma that had plagued Brooke for so many years couldn't be good for a pregnancy.

Michelle teetered on the brink of losing it. She hated crying. Hated that she even felt a need to cry. How much more selfish could she be?

She had to get away while she still could. Escape before all that hurt and self-admonishment came out on a rush of bitter tears. Turning on her bare feet, she slipped past the milling crowd and into the double patio doors, thankful she was alone. Thankful, for once, that her mother was occupied with Brooke and not playing chief cook and bottle washer.

Inside the ample kitchen a current of emotion swamped Michelle like a swollen river. So did the tears.

She allowed them only a moment before she started cleaning away the remnants of lunch like a mad maid on a ticking time clock. Like her mother. She scraped the paper plates clean into the disposal then threw them in the trash bin. She dumped liquid from myriad cups before tossing them into the overflowing sink. She picked up a plastic fork that had slipped from her hands and hurled it like a missile across the room where it landed near the dinette.

Slowly she walked to the table, grasped the back of one chair and knelt to pick up the utensil. She paused to swipe at her face damp with tears of frustration.

A pair of sandaled feet came into view. Two bare,

tanned legs dusted by dark masculine hair shot upward from the feet, thighs slightly exposed before being covered by blue swim trunks. Two equally well-defined, bronzed arms dangled at the sides of the trunks, attached to an all-male torso covered by a white tank top. As Michelle visually progressed past the strong column of his throat and on up to his brown eyes, she knew she was truly in dire straits.

It was *him.*

Of all the people to join her pity party, Nick Kempner would have been the last to receive an invitation.

She stood with the fork clutched in one palm, the other hand still braced on the chair. His trademark grin faltered when he met her gaze, and Michelle wished she could just dissolve into the puddles of pool water on the floor.

She was an emotional wreck, and he had the nerve to look sympathetic. Why, oh, why, hadn't she left an hour ago? What had she done to deserve Nick Kempner's compassion? And how in the heck was she going to explain?

Michelle didn't need to explain why she'd been crying, but Nick shored up for an explanation, anyway.

"You're here," she said, shattering his expectations.

"Yep, I'm here." He tugged a napkin from the stack set out on the end of the dining room table and handed it to her.

She hesitantly took it and dabbed at her eyes. "You probably think I've totally lost it."

No, but she was obviously distressed, and he wanted to know why. "Care to talk about it?"

She flipped the napkin clutched in her hand. "It's

nothing, really. Just the usual hormones. I'm feeling a little testy at the moment.''

He pointed to the towel slung low on her hips. "Do you have a weapon tucked away in there?''

At least that earned him a smile from her. "No, just this." She held up the plastic fork she'd been retrieving from the floor when he'd walked into the room.

He grinned. "I guess I should be grateful.''

She set the fork aside and asked, "Did you hear the news?''

"Nope. Just got here. What news?''

"Brooke's pregnant." She didn't sound happy.

Nick curled his hand on the back of the chair and leaned into it. "Well I'll be damned." He didn't dare tell her that Jared had informed him yesterday about the baby. Obviously, Michelle hadn't been afforded that courtesy.

He understood all too well how unexpected news could shake a person up. Case in point, Bridget's classic divorce-paper delivery at his office, the first he'd known about it. A lie. He'd known it was inevitable. He just hadn't wanted to deal with the possibility.

Yeah, he could relate to Michelle's anguish.

Michelle sniffed again. "Pretty incredible, huh?''

"Yeah. Pretty incredible. Do you want to sit down?''

He pulled back the chair from the table. Without a word she collapsed in it like a punctured balloon.

Taking the chair beside her, he scraped his mind trying to come up with something appropriate, something halfway consoling to say. He couldn't think of one damn thing.

Nick allowed her some silence and wondered if he should leave. Maybe she wanted to be alone. Maybe she needed to be held. He could do that, although with her wearing a bikini and a fresh set of tears, that probably wouldn't be a good idea. The tears affected him more than her lack of clothing at the moment. He hated to see a woman cry, and he figured a strong woman like Michelle Lewis didn't take emotional outbursts lightly. Neither did he. But he wasn't too good with comfort, at least not the kind she needed. Medicine had taught him that. Bridget had reminded him of that more times than he could shake a stick at.

The patio door slid open, and Jeanie Lewis, Brooke and Michelle's mother, stepped in with Nick's four-year-old daughter, Kelsey, braced on one hip. During those times Nick and Kelsey had joined the Grangers and Lewises for dinner the past few months, Kelsey had adopted Jeanie as a surrogate grandmother. Unfortunately for Nick, Michelle had never made it to those get-togethers, probably in avoidance of facing him after the wedding fiasco.

"Here he is, Kelsey," Jeanie said, then sent him a mother's smile. "She's been looking all over for you. Jared said you might be in here."

His daughter's eyes, much like his own, lit up with pure kid joy. "Look, Daddy. I'm gonna swim with Auntie Jeanie." She held out her arms, both wrapped in lemon-yellow floaties.

"You bet, punkin."

Nick stood, and Michelle turned in her chair to face her mother and Kelsey. Her smile was sincere. "That's a good-looking swimsuit, sweetie."

Kelsey looked down and rubbed a hand over the pink-and-green ruffled top. "Daddy got it."

"Really?" Michelle rose and turned her pretty face to Nick. "Daddy has really good taste."

Nick couldn't deny that. He more than appreciated Michelle's shiny blue number. He would appreciate it more if he could see the whole thing, but the bottom half was covered by the blasted towel. That would be easy to remedy with one flick of a finger at the loose knot.

He tried to dislodge thoughts of Michelle's bikini from his mind since his child was present. Not to mention Michelle's mother, who, he'd just bet, wouldn't take too kindly to him ogling her daughter.

Nick took Kelsey's hand into his, still fascinated by her perfect fingers, as he had been since the day she was born. "This is Michelle, kiddo."

Taking Kelsey's free hand, Michelle gave it a gentle shake. "It's nice to meet you, Kelsey. Are you having fun?"

Kelsey nodded with a definitive jerk of her head, sending her chestnut curls into a dance. Then she leaned over and cupped Michelle's cheek, taking Nick by surprise. Normally she was guarded with strangers, yet she seemed totally captivated by Michelle. He could relate to that.

"You're pretty," Kelsey said, surveying Michelle's face with open worship. The force of Michelle's responding, dimpled smile sent Nick's whole body reeling. The way she placed her hand over Kelsey's made him value this soft side of Michelle Lewis that much more.

"Not as pretty as you, sweetie," Michelle said. "You look like your daddy."

"Yeah. Like daddy."

Jeanie Lewis placed a kiss on Kelsey's face, leaving a pink lip imprint on her cheek. "This one's a doll,

Nick." She looked over Kelsey's head right at Michelle. "Shelly, are you all right?"

Michelle averted her eyes. "I'm fine, Mom."

"I think she's had too much sun," Nick said. "I'm making her sit awhile before she goes back out."

"Good idea. She's probably exhausted. She works much too hard." Jeanie continued to study Michelle as if trying to read her thoughts. "Isn't that some news about Brooke, Shelly? I didn't know what to say, especially with Brooke's asthma. But I guess it will all work out." She didn't sound too confident.

Kelsey squirmed in Jeanie's arms. "I wanna go now."

Nick bussed his daughter under the chin, for once glad the four-year-old had a limited attention span. "Anyone ever tell you patience is a virtue, kiddo?"

Jeanie slid Kelsey to her feet and took her hand. "I'll watch her, Nick. I need to get in some practice with a grandchild on the way." She patted her bobbed, silver hair and sent him a sunny smile that seemed strained. "You and Michelle have a nice visit."

"Thanks, Mrs. Lewis. I'll be out in a minute." He crouched down and framed Kelsey's sweet face in his palms. "You be a good girl." After popping a kiss on her chubby cheek, he straightened.

Kelsey sent Michelle a demure wave. "'Bye, Shelly."

Michelle's smile returned. "'Bye, Kelsey."

After Jeanie led his fidgeting daughter out the door, Nick faced Michelle again. She wrapped her arms low around her tanned midriff, but not before he caught a partial glimpse of her navel. Man, he'd give up his vacation to see the rest of it and all points below. Silently scolding himself for his wicked thoughts, he dragged his eyes back to her face.

"Your daughter's beautiful, Dr. Kempner."

So are you, he wanted to say. Instead he settled for, "I can only take half the credit. She is a great kid, though."

Michelle dropped her gaze to the floor. "Thanks for the explanation you handed my mother. I didn't want to upset her."

"No problem." He shifted his weight from one leg to the other. "She seems a little worried about Brooke."

Michelle finally raised her eyes to his. "She is. And with good cause."

"The asthma?"

"Yes. But as she said, I'm sure it will all work out."

Michelle didn't sound at all confident. Nick couldn't blame her. Although OB wasn't his thing, he suspected maintaining a pregnant asthmatic could have its challenges. But Brooke and Jared had overcome a lot of stumbling blocks to reach this milestone, and he figured this was only one more to overcome. At least they had each other to lean on.

A nagging heaviness settled on Nick's chest like an uninvited, long-lost cousin. He ignored it, choosing instead to focus on Michelle, now working her bottom lip with her teeth—a full bottom lip he could definitely enjoy kissing.

"Well, I guess I'm heading home now," she announced, cutting into his questionable thoughts.

He didn't want her to go, for many reasons. "Hey, I just got here. The party's only begun to get interesting."

She slicked a hand over her scalp and tightened her

ponytail. "I can only imagine. But that's all I'll be able to do since I need to get some work done."

"On a Sunday afternoon?"

"I brought some stuff home with me. Until this campaign's over, I'm not going to have much time to slack off."

"Are you sure? I make a mean margarita." He topped off the offer with a grin.

She tightened the towel at her waist and crossed her arms over her chest. "That sounds tempting, but I'll have to pass."

He wanted badly to smooth the worry from her face. Make her stay. "So they call you Shelly, huh?"

A slight blush tinged her cheeks. "Heavens, yes. Luckily no one calls me that at the hospital. Makes me feel like I'm Kelsey's age."

"Okay, so I'll just call you Michelle. And you can call me Nick." She would call him much worse if she knew the path his thoughts were taking. He couldn't seem to pull his eyes away from her face, had an even harder time keeping them away from her body, where he took a subtle mental inventory. The perfectly carved collarbone, the scoop of the bikini top that revealed ample cleavage, the slender torso, all painted a fascinating portrait of a fascinating woman.

"Well, Nick, I really do need to go. I'm so sleepy that if I stay, I'll probably have to find a bed."

If she stayed, he'd help her find one. And join her.

Releasing an exaggerated sigh to keep from groaning, he said, "Okay. But don't work too hard. Life is short. I've learned that lesson the hard way."

She reached for a canvas bag hanging on the back of a chair and slipped it over her slender shoulder. "How so?"

Man, that could take hours to explain. He wasn't up to baring his soul completely, so he'd give her an abbreviated version of the whole sorry story his life had been. "I missed out on a lot when Kelsey was a baby because of my work. And now I only get to see her every other weekend, so I guess you could say I'm still missing out."

"That's a shame, Nick." She sounded as if she meant it. As if she understood how badly he hated the part-time dad thing.

"Yeah, but that's just the way it is."

Michelle clutched the bag to her chest. At least now Nick could concentrate better on the conversation. "Can you ask for more time with her during the week?"

He had asked. About a thousand times. He was even willing to cut out of the office early. But Bridget wouldn't budge. She didn't want Kelsey exposed to "his women," as if he really had a revolving door in his two-bedroom apartment. Not that he hadn't indulged a time or two in female companionship. But it hadn't been that often, although the hospital scuttlebutt would say otherwise.

"Maybe someday my ex will allow me some extra time," he said. "After the battle scars start to fade."

"Tough divorce?"

"The toughest."

"It will all work out," she said wistfully.

Nick wasn't sure if Michelle spoke of his life or her own. She might appear confident on the exterior, but her vulnerabilities were showing. Not that she'd meant for him to see them. And damned if he didn't like what he saw. All of it. All of her. And he intended to see more.

Two

Nick had been waiting all afternoon to give Jared Granger a hefty dose of his own medicine and to ask him a few questions about Michelle Lewis.

"So how does it feel knowing you're going to be a dad, Granger? Knowing you're going to be responsible for this person for at least twenty years, worrying if you're screwing up—"

"Shut up, Kempner."

Jared made the warning through a proud-as-a-peacock grin while they stood near the barbecue pit as the party began to wind down.

Nick could identify with that smile. He'd worn exactly the same one when Bridget had told him she was pregnant five years ago, a time when he'd still held on to the hope that the marriage might survive since they would have a child to consider. Man, had he been wrong.

"Actually, I'm happy for you and Brooke," Nick said. "There's nothing like it in the world, being a dad." Even a part-time one, he thought as he watched Kelsey splashing around in the pool with Brooke's mom. Not that he didn't crave more time with his daughter.

Jared held up a beer for a toast. "Except maybe for finding the right woman to have that baby with."

Nick clicked his bottle against Jared's, experiencing a little sting of envy. "Yeah, looks like you got lucky the first time." If only he could say the same for himself.

Surveying the last of the guests, Nick was disappointed to find that Michelle had left after all. When he'd departed the kitchen to give her some space, he'd hoped she would change her mind. She certainly was changing his about her.

"So what do you know about Brooke's sister?" he asked, probably at his own detriment.

Jared's grin deepened, confirming Nick's concern. "Why? Are you still interested?"

Think fast, Kempner. "I talked to her in the kitchen a while ago. She was pretty upset over Brooke not telling her about the baby."

Jared's smile dropped out of sight. "I was afraid of that. But they'll work it out. They're pretty close."

"Yeah? They don't seem that much alike."

"In some ways they are. Michelle's pretty devoted to her career and her family. When she's not working, she's at her parents' house making sure they're okay."

"So she doesn't date?"

"You are interested, aren't you?"

He'd been caught with his mind in the proverbial

cookie jar. So much for being subtle. "Let's just say I'm mildly curious."

Jared let go a sharp laugh. "I'd wager you're mildly lustful. Michelle's a looker, all right. Seems to me she's anything but receptive to men right now."

"Yeah, why's that?"

Jared looked over his shoulder, probably visually patrolling for Brooke, then lowered his voice. "Brooke told me she's been fairly unlucky with relationships. She had one that went pretty sour a couple of years back."

"Haven't we all."

"To my way of thinking, after your argument with her at our wedding, that makes your odds slim to none."

Obviously, they had drawn more attention during their confrontation than Nick had first believed. "It wasn't an argument exactly." More like casual warfare. "We just don't see eye to eye on certain things."

"Let me guess. You asked her for a date and she refused."

"Nope. I just told her she looked like a princess in her bridesmaid's dress, and then she said if I thought she believed in that old fairy tale about kissing a toad, I had another think coming even if I did fit the bill, at which time I made a comparison to her and the ice sculpture. That was about it."

Jared chuckled. "That was enough."

"Yeah, maybe, but I was just trying to be nice."

"You were trying to hit on her."

"Not exactly true." Close, but not exactly.

Jared sent a wave in Brooke's direction and gave her a look that revealed a man too smitten for his own good. He finally turned his attention back to Nick. "Let me tell you something else about Michelle Lewis. She's a beautiful woman who probably fights off a dozen come-ons a week. Maybe even a day. If you want to win her over, you're going to have to rethink your usual 'Hi, I'm Nick, I want you.'"

"That's a low blow, Granger. I have more class than that."

Nick immediately recalled Al Rainey's obvious lust for Michelle and realized Jared was probably right about men hitting on her frequently and without regard to restraint. God knew that was old Al in a nutshell. And yes, Nick wasn't always subtle. But he was good at picking up signals, and he knew when to back off.

Nick felt the overwhelming need to defend himself, probably because he had spent much of his time in recent days on guard where his ex and her accusations about other women were concerned. "First of all I'm not really looking for anything heavy. Secondly, I'm not the playboy everyone makes me out to be. And last, who needs the grief of a woman who's not the least bit interested in men at the moment?"

"You do. You thrive on challenge. You live for it." Jared nailed him with a serious glare. "But I'll warn you. Michelle is a really nice woman beneath that all-business exterior. Basically your average girl-next-door type."

If Michelle Lewis was a girl next door, then Nick was Albert Einstein. "Are you saying I'm not her type?"

"I'm saying that if you do anything to hurt her, you'll have to answer to Brooke, and believe me, you don't want to deal with her."

Nick realized all too well the potency of sisterly ties. He was the baby in a family with three female siblings.

He'd barely survived all that womanly camaraderie. Not to mention the lack of bathroom space. "Okay. *If* I decide I might want to give Michelle Lewis a shot, I'll proceed with caution."

"I'm not betting on that horse."

Jared knew him all too well. Yeah, he did thrive on challenge, but was Michelle Lewis worth the trouble? Whatever did transpire between them, he would definitely make sure he wasn't the one to get burned.

But somehow Nick knew that when he was around Michelle Lewis, he was already standing too close to the fire.

As it was now nearing lunchtime, Michelle decided to take a break from her work and make the call she'd needed to make since yesterday. She needed to apologize to Brooke for her harried departure from the party. She also needed answers as to why Brooke hadn't told her sooner about the baby. Maybe something was wrong aside from Brooke's asthma. Something Brooke hadn't told her yet. That prospect frightened her. She couldn't stand the thought of something happening to her little sister.

"Hey. You got a minute?"

Michelle's grip tightened on the phone at the sound of that voice—a voice belonging to a doctor she had thought about much too often in the past twenty-four hours. She couldn't seem to get him out of her head. She certainly didn't need him in her office, invading her space at work and worming his way back into her stubborn psyche.

Michelle dropped the phone onto its cradle and stared up at Nick Kempner's disarming smile. She glanced at the door he had managed to close behind him without her noticing. She was trapped in a small room with a man who emitted sensuality like a nuclear-powered aphrodisiac.

On the heels of his surprise appearance, she was amazed she found her voice. "Good afternoon, Dr. Kempner. What brings you to the administrative offices?"

Without an invitation he pulled back the chair in front of her desk and sat, one leg crossed over the other as if he planned to settle in for a while. "I have a question for you."

The doctor looked much too good in his tailored white shirt and conservative blue tie, his shiny brown hair as slick as his smile. Not that he hadn't looked great in swim trunks.

Get a grip, Michelle. "Okay. What is it?"

His grin expanded. "Just say yes."

"Yes to—"

"Good. I'll pick you up at seven."

The man was incorrigible. And sexier than any man had a right to be. "Tonight?" That wasn't at all what she'd intended to say. And she darned sure didn't mean to say it with such enthusiasm.

"No. Saturday night. I figured since we're both attending the fund-raising gala, we might as well go together. Unless you already have a date."

"I'm not going."

His dark brows drew down over his equally dark eyes. "What do you mean you're not going? This thing's supposed to raise money for your pet project."

Exactly what Michelle's assistant had said when she'd asked her to fill in at the gala. "Actually, I'm going to the reception with the benefactors that afternoon. But I'm not going to the dance that night."

"Care to tell me why?"

No, she didn't, at least not the whole truth—that a few years back she'd met a doctor at a similar event who, little had she known at the time, belonged to someone else. "Large crowds aren't exactly my cup of tea."

"Mine, either. But I'm required to put in an appearance. I assumed you would be, too."

"Not this time. I need to continue working on finalizing the ad layouts. Besides, no one will even miss me."

"I will."

Darn him. And darn her renegade smile that picked that exact moment to come out of hiding. She willed it away. "I appreciate that, Dr. Kempner, but I'm afraid you'll have to find someone else to escort."

"What if I don't want to escort anyone else?"

She stacked some papers that didn't need stacking, in avoidance of his tempting eyes. "There are probably, say, four single male doctors in this hospital and about ten times as many unattached women. That makes the odds in your favor. So I'm sure you can find someone who would more than appreciate your company."

"And you don't?" He slumped lower in the chair. "Man, you really know how to hurt a guy."

In all honesty she did appreciate his company. More than she should. Not that she would ever make that confession, especially to him. "Let's just say I'm not looking for companionship at the moment."

She glanced up and met his intense stare. "What *are* you looking for, Michelle?"

Not the kind of trouble he was offering. She didn't have time to date, and with her lousy track record with

gorgeous doctors who were much too compelling for
their own good, she didn't have the desire, either.
"Success in my work and taking care of my family,
first and foremost."

He leaned forward, giving Michelle a lethal dose of
his cologne and a good look at his serious expression.
"That won't keep you warm at night."

"I manage okay."

"I'm sure you do. Or at least you think you do. But
take it from me, after a while burying yourself in your
work won't give you the satisfaction you need. And
your family can only offer you so much comfort."

"And what satisfaction are you referring to?" Did
she really just ask such a thing?

His smile made another grandstand appearance.
"The kind that makes you really feel alive, and believe
me, you won't find that in ad layouts or Sunday din-
ners."

Michelle abruptly stood, looking for an escape from
his truths. Looking for a way out from underneath all
the heat the man was generating in her turncoat body.
"Well, right now I have a lot of *satisfying* work to do,
so I'll see you out on my way to the copy room."

She grabbed up the papers that didn't need copying
and quickly moved from behind her desk, but the doctor was much quicker.

He stood by the door, one hand braced on the facing,
the other hidden away in his trouser pocket. She
grasped the doorknob, but before she could turn it, he
said, "There's one more thing I need to say."

She dropped her hand from the knob and faced him
with the papers clutched against her chest. "What?"

"Speaking as a doctor, you need to get some rest.
You look tired."

A nice way of putting she looked like pond scum. "Your advice is duly noted."

He took his hand from his pocket and traced a path underneath her eyes with one sturdy fingertip. "Dark smudges. Looks like you're not getting much sleep."

She probably wouldn't sleep tonight, either. But work wouldn't be standing in her way. He would. Right now an invigorating stream of warmth flowed from where his fingertip had been all the way down to places that weren't tired at all. In fact, they were totally alert and making themselves known.

Fumbling in her blazer pocket, she withdrew her glasses and slipped them on. "Now you don't have to look at them."

"I'm serious, Michelle." If his expression was any indication, he was.

"Okay. I'll take a nap. Would that appease you, Doctor?"

"It's a start. And I wish you would call me Nick."

She had once, a poor move on her part. First names denoted intimacy, and she couldn't afford to have that with someone so terribly hard to resist. "Since we're in the office, I think it's best we maintain a professional relationship."

He grinned. "So you're saying you'll call me Nick when we're not in the office?"

"I'm saying...actually..." She was rambling like an idiot, all because of him. "Don't you have something to fix? Maybe a broken leg or two or three?"

He dropped his hand from the door and checked his watch. "Yeah. As a matter of fact, I'm late for my next surgery."

"Don't let me keep you from your work."

His smoldering smile returned. "You already have,

but it was well worth the lost time.'' He bent closer and whispered, ''That's the kind of satisfaction I've learned to appreciate.''

Michelle stared at the ringing telephone sitting on the end table next to her favorite lounge chair. She needed to answer but hesitated. For some reason she worried that maybe Nick Kempner was calling. If so, she worried more that she might find herself agreeing to something she had no business agreeing to, namely going with him to the gala. He had shaken her up today like an out-of-control blender. She'd barely been able to concentrate on her work.

Why couldn't she get him off her mind? Because he had more magnetism than a televangelist, that's why. But it wasn't just his charisma. Beneath that magnetic facade, she sensed true caring. She'd seen it at Brooke's when he'd offered her consolation and again another glimpse of it in her office today when he'd voiced his concern about her health. And he was so gentle with his daughter. But that wasn't quite enough to persuade her to give in to his charms. She had done that once with another charmer; she didn't intend to do it again.

On the fourth ring she finally answered.

''Hey, sis, where'd you go yesterday in such a hurry?''

The call Michelle would have made herself had it not been for Nick Kempner's untimely appearance.

Michelle gripped the phone with all the hurt she had felt since the backyard barbecue. ''I needed to get out of there.''

''Was it that bad?''

Not all of it. Nick crept into her thoughts like some

panther on the prowl. She willed him to disappear, at least for the time being. "Actually, it was okay. I just had some work to do at home."

"You're mad at me for not telling you about the baby, aren't you?"

The remorse in Brooke's tone helped to ease Michelle's hurt, but it didn't completely go away.

"I'm disappointed, Brooke. I hated learning about the baby as if I'm some casual acquaintance. Why didn't you say something sooner?"

"I tried to tell you last Friday evening, but you were still at work. I even left a message on your cell phone voice mail for you to call. I never heard from you. And then you came late to the party and there just wasn't enough time or the opportunity."

All valid reasons, Michelle decided. Valid reasons for Brooke not telling her this past weekend. "True, I haven't checked my private voice mail in a couple of days. But why didn't you tell me after you found out?"

"Because I knew you'd be worried about me. You know how you get when it comes to my health, especially with the asthma. I wanted to make sure enough time had passed so you'd know that everything's fine."

Michelle couldn't deny that she was concerned. More than concerned. "Of course I'm going to worry. You're my baby sister. But you have to know how happy I am for you and Jared."

"I do know that, and please understand I never meant to hurt you, Shelly. This was just something Jared and I agreed upon, waiting until I was at least in my second trimester."

Second trimester? "When is this baby due?"

"October twenty-ninth."

Michelle did a mental countdown. "You're begin-

ning your third trimester, Brooke. How is that possible?
You're barely showing.''

"Mom told me she didn't show until the later
months so I guess I've inherited that from her. But I
really can't believe you didn't notice my, shall we say,
blossoming figure.''

With Michelle's recent work schedule and her visits
with her parents, she hadn't been around Brooke all
that much in recent months to notice. Besides, Michelle
had a knack for being oblivious to certain things.
"Well, I did notice you're looking a bit more healthy
than normal, and that you're wearing baggier clothes,
but I thought that went along with being happily married.''

Brooke laughed. "Heavens, I hope not. I hope it's
the pregnancy that's necessitated a Wide Load sign
across my butt, not my marriage.''

Michelle joined in the laughter for a few moments
before her concern for Brooke's health again kicked in.
"What about the asthma?''

"I'm doing fine with that. My doctor's watching it
closely. I'm getting by without much medication. We'll
just hope for the best.''

Brooke, always the optimist. Michelle wished she
could be as sanguine, but she had witnessed Brooke's
asthma when it had been at its worst. So many times
Michelle had wished she could take it all away from
her sister. She still did, but that wasn't possible, then
or now. She would simply offer all her support to
Brooke and pray everything turned out okay.

"Okay, Brookie, I guess you and Jared know what
you're doing. Obviously you do, or you wouldn't be
pregnant.''

"Cut it out, Shelly. You're making me blush.''

"Yeah, right. What would make you blush would blister a metal wash pot."

"True. After living with Jared, I think I'm about all blushed out."

Michelle experienced a tug of envy. What would it be like to have a man love you as completely as Jared loved Brooke? What would it be like to have a child with that man?

Nick Kempner hopped into Michelle's brain once again like an annoying grasshopper. Or a frog. Why did she keep thinking about him? Men like Nick and commitment were not necessarily synonymous. Not that she wanted a commitment anytime soon. Or at least that wasn't what she'd planned—

"Are you still there, Shelly?"

"Yeah, still here."

"Mom said you were talking to Nick at the party."

Michelle cringed, thinking she had somehow blurted out his name unconsciously. "Why on earth did you bring that up?"

"Jared told me he's really interested in you."

Interested in rattling her proverbial chain, Michelle thought. She had definitely been prisoner to his espresso eyes and high-voltage grin that afternoon. But only for a moment. Okay, a few moments. "Is there a point to this, Brooke?"

"Nick's a decent guy, Shelly. A great dad, too. You might want to give him a chance."

"I've got enough going on with mom and dad, my job—"

"Admit it. You're afraid to get too close to anyone."

And with good reason, Michelle decided. "Don't you dare try your hand at matchmaking again. If you recall, you did that already and it was a disaster."

"You're not going to let me forget that, are you? I didn't know Brett was married when I introduced you two."

"Neither did he. At least he didn't act like it." And neither had Michelle until it had been too late. Until she had invested a lot of time and emotions in a relationship that could never be.

"Point taken," Brooke said. "But does one bad experience have to spoil everything? Take me, for instance. If I hadn't opened myself up again, I wouldn't be married to Jared now. You were the one who encouraged me to go for it. I honestly believe there's someone out there for you, too. Someone who's your type and can make you happy."

Michelle couldn't find it in her heart to believe it. "Maybe I don't have a type, Brooke."

Brooke sighed. "Maybe you're not looking in the right place."

Michelle was basically tired of looking. Besides, her current celibate lifestyle held certain advantages, the least of which was not having to sort through the man pile to find that gem of a guy. She doubted he existed, at least for her.

"I don't want anything serious, Brooke."

"Who says you have to consider anything serious? What about living for the moment? Why don't you try Nick out, see where it goes?"

"I can't have just a fling." Michelle didn't relish the thought of keeping emotions totally out of it. It seemed to work for men—Brett included, and more than likely Nick—but she wasn't sure it would ever work for her.

"Admit it," Brooke said, "you're scared to have fun, and you know that Nick Kempner would probably be lots of fun."

Michelle was scared to get involved at the risk of getting her heart trampled. "Nick Kempner's as fast as a race-car driver and he would probably lose me in the first turn."

"I honestly believe you could hold your own with him."

Oh, brother, or sister in this case. "Enough, Brooke."

Brooke released a sigh of defeat. "Okay, I'll lay off. I need to get to bed, anyway. Jared's waiting for me."

"That doesn't sound conducive to rest."

"Maybe not, but what a way to lose sleep. The man is insatiable. But then, so am I. Pregnancy does crazy things to a woman's hormones, let me tell you."

This time Michelle's face burned. "I don't want all the torrid details, so go to bed."

"One more thing. Did you change your mind about going to the gala?"

First Nick, now Brooke. "I'm not in the mood for dancing."

"Then do you mind baby-sitting at our house? We're planning to go with a few friends, and we could use someone to stay with the kids. We can have everyone meet over here, since our place is bigger than your apartment."

What a relief that Brooke hadn't lit into another lecture on how Michelle needed to get out more. "How many are you expecting to be there?"

The way Brooke paused to clear her throat, Michelle expected an army of feisty two-year-olds. Instead Brooke said, "Only one right now, but there could be more. It will give you some practice playing aunt."

Michelle didn't need any practice. Five years Brooke's senior, she'd diapered and changed Brooke, cared for her like the "little mother" for as long as she could remember. Still, she did love kids and wouldn't mind spending her Saturday evening with a few. Much less complicated than spending time trying to second-guess a man. "Okay. Sounds like fun. I'll be over around six."

"Great. You're the best."

"And don't you forget it," Michelle teased.

"I gather I'm forgiven for not telling you about the baby."

"Of course. I'll always forgive you no matter what you do."

Three

"**B**rooke Lewis Granger, I may never forgive you for this," Michelle muttered as she peeked through her sister's living room curtain.

Striding up Brooke and Jared's walkway was none other than Nick Kempner, dressed in black tie and accompanied by his daughter, obviously Michelle's charge for the evening. She adored Kelsey and didn't mind one bit baby-sitting the little girl. However, she did mind the fact that she would have to face the girl's father, especially since he looked like a young version of James Bond with his tanned face contrasting the white tuxedo shirt, his dark hair primed to perfection. At the moment the doctor was definitely shaking *and* stirring her belly.

Kelsey stood by his side, jerking his arm up and down like an old-fashioned well pump handle. Without regard for his neatly combed hair and perfectly pressed tuxedo, he grabbed her up and hoisted her onto his shoulders. She patted his head as if to say, Good boy.

Michelle backed away from the window and paced the room, letting go a string of mild curses aimed at her sister's continued secrecy.

When the doorbell rang, Michelle simply stared at the entrance. It rang once again but before she spurred herself into action, Brooke appeared wearing a robe.

"Are you going to get it, Shelly?"

"Are you going to explain why you didn't tell me I was sitting for Nick Kempner's daughter?"

Brooke had the gall to play innocent. "You didn't ask."

"Where are the rest of the kids?"

Brooke's gaze slid away. "Uh, actually, everyone else has sitters, so it's just Kelsey. Nick was the only one in a bind."

Nick wasn't the only one, Michelle thought. Nowhere to run, nowhere to hide. And she got the distinct feeling this was another one of Brooke's subtle attempts at more matchmaking.

Without further comment Brooke opened the door to allow Nick entry while Michelle hung back right behind the opening to the den. She moved inside the room to where she could still see Nick, but Nick couldn't see her. Enough distance to allow her the opportunity to get a good look at him without him knowing it. And what a view it was.

Whomever he'd decided to escort tonight, she was one lucky girl. Michelle battled the sudden jealousy, knowing she had no right to feel that way. After all, she had turned Nick down.

Kelsey rushed in like a tempest and grabbed Brooke around the knees.

"Whoa, Cisco," Nick said. "Be careful with Aunt Brooke. She's going to have a baby, remember?"

Kelsey looked up at her dad and stuck out a defiant chin. "I'm Kelsey not Cisco."

Nick reached down and ruffled her curls. "I don't care if your name is mud, you still need to be careful."

With an awe-filled expression, Kelsey stood on tiptoes and patted Brooke's belly. "Hi, baby!"

Smiling, Brooke said, "Baby says hi to you, too."

"I don't hear baby," Kelsey stated with a four-year-old's certainty.

Nick grabbed Kelsey back up into his arms. "Only mommies can hear babies when they're still in their tummies."

"And daddies, too," Michelle added, deciding she might as well join in and get it over with.

Nick glanced from Kelsey to Michelle, shock splashed all over his gorgeous face. "Michelle? What are you doing here?" He slowly lowered Kelsey to her feet. "Did you change your mind about the gala?"

She looked down at her ragged cutoffs and sloppy T-shirt. "Yeah, right. This is the latest in evening wear. Chic grunge. Do you like it?"

He gave her a lingering once-over and a slow-burn smile. "Works for me."

She should have known better than to ask his opinion. "Actually, I have a date with your daughter this evening."

Brooke took the opportunity to announce, "I'll go see if Jared's ready. And they say women take too long in the bathroom." She scurried around the corner in record time to make her escape.

"You're the baby-sitter?" The shock had returned to Nick's face and resounded in his tone.

Obviously, Michelle wasn't the only one left in the dark. "Yes, I'm the sitter. And if you're worried about that, I can give you references."

"I don't need any references. I trust you. I just thought you had work to do."

"I do, but it can wait until after Kelsey goes to bed, in case you're worried I'll neglect her for my layouts." She knelt at Kelsey's level and pointed to her left toward the sofa table sitting in the middle of the den. "There's some fresh-baked cookies over there, Kelsey. You can have one if Daddy says it's okay."

Kelsey stared up at Nick. "'Kay, Daddy?"

"Sure. But save some for me."

"'Kay." Kelsey headed toward the treat, leaving Nick and Michelle alone to face off.

"Maybe I should change my plans," he said after a few moments of silence.

"Then you don't trust me."

"I'm not saying that. I just thought it might be nice to have a visit. Me, you and Kelsey." He heavily emphasized the "me" and "you" part.

"Why? And waste a good tuxedo rental?"

"I own it."

He would. "Oh. But I'm sure your presence will be greatly missed," she added, trying to discourage him from making good on his suggestion. She didn't trust herself to be alone with him, even with his child present. Children eventually went to sleep. Unfortunately, her unwelcome attraction to him might not.

He rubbed his clean-shaven jaw, looking thoughtful and incredibly debonair. "I'm not sure anyone would miss me exactly, but I have promised a few people I'd be there."

Michelle wanted to ask what people in particular.

Did he mean just one, namely his date? She had the strongest urge to go back to the window to see if he had a woman waiting for him in the car. She didn't recall seeing anyone, but then, he probably had yet to pick her up, whoever "her" might be. Michelle sorted through a mental laundry list of all the possibilities and hated herself for doing it.

"You ready to go, Kempner?"

Michelle turned to find Brooke and Jared walking toward them hand in hand, looking like models for domestic bliss. Jared, too, was dressed in a tux, Brooke decked out in a blue chiffon flowing gown that did little to hide her pregnancy. Guess she didn't need to hide it anymore, Michelle thought, the hurt again trying to surface. She refused to let it.

"I'm ready if you are." Nick gave Michelle his smile. "Have fun with the kid. She'll probably be asleep before nine. She likes cartoons."

"Nice to know," Michelle said. "But I brought some supplies for finger painting. And some books."

His grin deepened. "You know something, I've always wanted to try my hand at finger painting, no pun intended."

Michelle found herself smiling, too. "If we have any paint left over, we'll save it for you."

"Great. Then maybe we can play when I get back."

That almost sounded like a promise to Michelle. A sensual promise, one she shouldn't even consider in spite of the fact that she had images of applying paint to Nick Kempner's body in some very creative ways.

Jared cleared his throat, slapping Michelle back into reality. "If you two are through discussing your social schedule for the evening, do you think maybe we can go now, Kempner?"

Nick took his sweet time tearing his gaze from Michelle. "Yeah. But I'll take my own car in case I want to leave early."

Or in case he wanted to take his date somewhere secluded, Michelle decided, trying hard to tamp down another spurt of jealousy. She had no call to be jealous. It could very well be her, if she had only said yes. But she hadn't, and for some reason she almost regretted that decision. Almost.

"Suit yourself," Jared said. "We still need to get out of here."

"I hear you, Granger. Just let me kiss my girl goodbye."

For the briefest moment Michelle thought he'd meant her. For the briefest moment she wished he had.

Instead he made his way into the den and leaned down to kiss Kelsey's cheek that was now covered in chocolate measles. "Be good, kiddo. Daddy will be back in a little while."

"In a little while," Kelsey repeated then licked her sticky fingers before rubbing them down her light-blue overalls.

Nick brushed past the threesome and headed to the door, but not before facing Michelle again. "Brooke's got some extra nightclothes for Kelsey in the guest room. If you don't mind giving her a bath, then I can pick her up and take her home without having to wake her."

"No, I don't mind at all. That's what I'm here for."

He winked. "You be good, too, Michelle." With that he was gone in a rush, leaving Michelle pleasantly warm all over in reaction to the sultry way he'd said her name.

"I've got my pager on if you need us," Jared told her.

What Michelle needed at the moment was a Nick Kempner antidote. "Thanks. Hopefully I won't have to use it."

Brooke gave her a quick hug. "We won't be too terribly late. My ankles are starting to swell. I might not make it past eleven in these darned heels."

Jared slipped an arm around her waist. "I'll give you a good foot massage when we get home. How does that sound?"

"Yummy," Brooke said with a smile meant solely for him. They left with only a brief wave directed at Michelle, arm in arm, heart in heart.

Michelle locked and bolted the door, then leaned back against it with a sigh.

"Well, Kelsey, looks like it's just you and me." *At least until your daddy returns.*

As much as she hated to admit it, Michelle couldn't wait for Kelsey's daddy to return. Not because she didn't want to be around Kelsey. The little girl was a breath of fresh air, a wake-up call for Michelle as to what was really important in life. Her impatience for Nick's reappearance had more to do with desire. A very unhealthy desire, at that.

Wanting Nick Kempner was unhealthy. Sort of like consuming too much cholesterol-laden food. Tastes great at the moment, but silently detrimental to one's well-being.

Especially the heart.

All Nick Kempner wanted at the moment was to get away from the requisite schmoozing and the deafening band. He tugged at his collar, nearly suffocating from the bow tie's noose.

Surveying the hotel ballroom, he finally caught sight of Jared and Brooke engaged in a conversation with none other than Al Rainey. At least the man had brought his lovely wife for a change.

Pushing his way through the chaos, a stifling mixture of expensive cologne and obvious arrogance, Nick finally reached Jared's side, unfortunately drawing Al Rainey's attention.

"Dr. Kempner, glad you could join us," Rainey said, his voice rising over the din, his tone less than welcoming.

Nick took the hand he offered and with forced courtesy said, "Good to see you."

"I don't believe you know my wife, Gabriella," Rainey said.

Nick wondered if the same held true for Al. Did *he* really know his wife? The woman looked nervous and somewhat self-conscious when she held her hand out.

"Nice to meet you, Mrs. Rainey," Nick said with a polite nod as he gave her hand a gentle shake.

Her smile shot up from the corners of her thin lips as if it were an automatic reflex. "And nice to meet you, Dr. Kempner."

She looked as though she wanted to disappear into the masses, or the carpet. She seemed as uncomfortable as Nick felt, probably hating this whole scene as much as he did.

Nick turned to Jared and declared, "I'm leaving."

"So soon?" Jared replied.

"Yeah. I need to get back to Kelsey."

"Don't you mean you need to get back to her sitter?"

Nick's glance shot to Brooke, who was thankfully conversing with the Raineys. "I don't have that much time with my daughter. No need to waste more at this shindig."

"If you say so."

"Are you guys going home anytime soon?"

Jared grinned. "I figure we'll be here at least another hour. Will that give you enough time?"

"For what?" Nick asked, although he didn't have to. He knew exactly what Jared was hinting at.

"Enough time to visit with Michelle."

"I told you I'm going to see Kelsey."

Jared checked his watch. "It's almost ten. Shouldn't Kelsey already be asleep?"

"Maybe, but she might not be. I'll take that chance."

"What other chances are you going to take, Kempner?"

"Lay off, Granger."

"Okay. Have a nice visit with your *daughter*." Jared laughed, a little too loudly in Nick's opinion.

Nick turned away in search of the nearest exit and freedom. But Sandra Allen, a redheaded R.N. as good at her job as she was at relentless pursuit, thwarted his departure.

Sandra tossed her auburn hair over one shoulder and sent him a devious smile. "Why, Nick Kempner, you're looking rather sharp this evening. Who's the lucky girl who has you all to herself tonight?"

"I'm alone." Nick immediately regretted making that admission when he saw Sandra's female radar light up her catlike eyes. Eyes that assessed him as if he were a choice mutual fund in need of an investor.

"Alone?" She laid a hand on her breast where ample cleavage showed like a beacon beneath the low-cut neckline of her dress. "I don't believe it."

"Believe it." He homed in on the nearby double doors, sensing escape was close at hand if he made his move, and fast. "I'm on my way out to pick up my daughter from the sitter's. Nice seeing you again, Sandra."

The woman had more tenacity than Kelsey when she wanted something badly enough, and from the come-on look spreading across her face, Nick had no doubt what she wanted.

"Well, Nick, I just happen to be alone, too." She looped her arm through his. "And I really think that's a shame. Perhaps you should give your sitter a call and tell her you've been detained for a while. We can be at my place in twenty minutes."

Nick could just imagine calling Michelle and letting her know that he was currently occupied with an insatiable nurse who had loving on her mind. "Sorry. Not tonight." Not ever again.

"Is there something I can do to persuade you?" She slipped one arm around his waist and brushed up against him. All of him. Subtlety was not one of Sandra's stronger suits. And although he had no intention of leaving with her, Nick's body stirred at the contact. He couldn't help it. He was only a man, and it had been a while since he'd been with a woman.

For the sake of diplomacy, and to avoid a scene, he took a much-needed step back and withdrew Sandra's arm. "Thanks, but I need to get back to my daughter."

The nurse looked more than a little miffed. "Okay. Suit yourself. Give me a call if you change your mind."

He wouldn't be changing his mind. "Have a nice night."

She turned and made her way back through the crowd, probably looking for another victim, Nick decided. The woman had never seemed all that selective when it came to men, one other reason why he hadn't considered a serious relationship with her.

As he pushed through the double doors, Nick couldn't help but question the sudden change in his attitude. He had been offered a night of mindless sex. A sure thing. Maybe at another time in the not-so-distant past he would have taken Sandra up on her offer. Maybe he would have settled solely for a meaningless relationship that was relatively uncomplicated. Nothing beyond physical need, a way to forget old recriminations and hurts. But that was then, and this was now. That prospect didn't hold any appeal.

He opted to return to Michelle, not even remotely a sure thing. It didn't really matter. What he wanted most from Michelle Lewis was her company. He enjoyed the banter. He wanted to get to know her. She was an enigma and, yeah, somewhat of a challenge.

But more important, she was a woman who knew what she wanted. Although he had seen her vulnerabilities, he found her self-confidence refreshing, not overbearing like Sandra's. And unlike Bridget, she was someone who didn't give in to insecurity and jealousy. Someone who wasn't content to remain invisible, unlike Gabriella Rainey. She would understand Nick's passion for his job because she felt that same passion for hers. She also liked his daughter, a big plus.

Yeah, Michelle Lewis was someone he definitely wanted to get to know better. *If* he could convince her that he was a man worth knowing.

* * *

Halfway up the Grangers' walkway, Nick paused in his tracks. A scene played out from behind the den's picture window facing the street. A scene that tugged at his heart and called up emotions long since vacant from his life.

On the ecru leather sofa sat Kelsey curled up at Michelle's side, Michelle's arm draped around her in a protective embrace, an open book sprawled in their laps, both sound asleep. Both looking like the portrait of peace.

Dealing with the likes of Sandra Allen earlier had convinced Nick of what he didn't want. Seeing Michelle curled up with his daughter confirmed to him that Michelle was special. She deserved the utmost respect. Although he couldn't deny that he wanted her, Nick was determined to show her that he was honorable in his intentions—starting tonight.

Nick hated to wake them, but he had no choice. He rapped his knuckles quietly on the door, hoping to rouse Michelle and not his daughter. After a time he heard footsteps padding into the entry. A sudden surge of excitement hurtled through him. A teenage kind of thrill, one that he needed to keep in check.

The door slowly opened to Michelle rubbing her eyes as though she couldn't quite focus. Either that or she didn't believe it was him. "You're back already?"

"Yeah. Two hours of back patting and mutual admiration was about all I could stand."

She sniffed and pushed stray hairs from her forehead. Her ponytail was a bit lopsided and a whole lot endearing to Nick. "Two hours? What time is it?"

"A little after ten."

She hung on to the door with both hands. "Really?"

"Really. Mind if I come in?"

Her face flushed and she stepped back. "Sorry. I'm kind of out of it."

She was kind of cute, in Nick's opinion. Her sparse makeup, ragged clothing and messy hair held a lot of appeal for a man who had recently endured uptight, stiff-coiffed women with fake smiles.

"Quiet," she said with a finger to her lips, then gestured for him to follow.

He walked behind her down the hallway toward the kitchen, glancing into the den, noting that Michelle had laid Kelsey on the couch and covered her with a pink crocheted throw.

He brought his gaze back to Michelle's long legs, bare to his eyes, sheer torment on his body. The cutoffs were short, at least on her. On someone Brooke's size, they might have been thigh length. But on Michelle, they hit just below her bottom—a bottom that was way too enticing for Nick not to notice.

Once in the breakfast room, Michelle turned to face him. "Want some cookies? We saved you a couple."

Nick leaned against the dinette table and glanced at the plate. He wasn't at all hungry for cookies. He was starving for Michelle. Determined to maintain a hold on his questionable appetite, he told her, "Yeah, I'll have a cookie. Got any coffee?"

"I can make a pot, I guess. I'm going to need a lot in order to stay awake a few more hours to get some work done."

Nick started to scold her and tell her she needed to go to bed and get some sleep. On afterthought, he decided to subtly work that issue into their conversation later. He didn't want to make her hostile right out of the gate.

While he finished off the cookie, Michelle plopped a filter into the coffeemaker then rummaged around in an overhead cabinet, arms stretched upward, taking the T-shirt in the same direction, giving Nick a great view of her great butt.

She pulled down the can of coffee, scooped some into the filter then grabbed the glass canister. "How did your date feel about you bugging out so early?"

Obviously she didn't get it. "I didn't have a date."

The glass pot fell out of her grasp and rolled into the sink without breaking. Michelle retrieved it without looking back. "Really?"

"You sound stunned."

"I am."

"I told you I didn't want to take anyone but you."

She tossed a glance at him over one shoulder while filling the canister with water from the sink. "I didn't realize you were serious about that."

He stepped closer to the cabinet, keeping a safe distance, both for her sake and his. "Why wouldn't you think I was serious?"

She shrugged. "Well, considering your reputation with women, I just assumed—"

"Don't assume anything about me, Michelle." He hadn't meant to sound so angry, but he despised this so-called reputation everyone kept throwing up in his face.

After turning on the coffeemaker, she faced him. "Sorry. I didn't mean to make assumptions."

He didn't want to get into this tonight with her, yet he needed her to understand that he wasn't the playboy doctor he'd been painted to be. "Since the divorce, there have been a couple of women. But nothing serious, and nothing sordid, as some would like to believe.''

He decided now was the time to execute a subject change. "How was Kelsey?"

Michelle's dimpled smile surfaced. "An angel of the first order. She's so smart. And funny. We had a great time. At least I did."

In Nick's opinion, Michelle's smile pretty much qualified her as angelic. "I imagine she had a great time, too." He imagined having his own great time with Michelle.

He reminded himself to be patient. In order for her to believe that he had more than an ounce of honor, he had to give her a barrel of space.

He leaned against the counter, but not too close to her. He wasn't that strong. "You really like kids, don't you?"

"Yes, I really do."

"Then you must be looking forward to your new niece or nephew."

"Of course." She grabbed up a dishcloth and began absently swiping at the cabinets. "I'm glad to hear I didn't miss anything by not going to the gala."

Her switch of subjects was as smooth as his. Obviously, she still hadn't quite accepted the news of Brooke's pregnancy, and that concerned Nick. Another subject he wanted to broach at some point in time, but not now. Not until she was ready to talk about it. "I sure could've used you as my dance partner."

Her smile slowly returned as she draped the rag over the sink's ledge and faced him. "Brooke wouldn't dance with you?"

"Jared had her occupied most of the night. They might as well be joined at the hip."

She sighed. "I know what you mean. I barely see her these days. But I guess that's what true love's all about, right?"

He wouldn't know. "Right."

Now seemed as good a time as any to ask something he had considered all the way home. "Do you think you might want to have dinner with me and Kelsey sometime?" He would prefer to have her all to himself, but he realized she might feel safer with his daughter along.

She threaded her bottom lip between her teeth. "Do you really think that's such a great idea?"

"Why not? It would give us the opportunity to get to know each other better."

"Why would you want to get to know me?"

That threw him mentally off balance. "Kind of a strange question. Do you think I have an ulterior motive?"

"Do you?"

He inched a little closer. "What do you think?"

"I have no idea, that's why I'm asking you."

He reached out and tucked behind her ear a few stray strands of silky dark hair that had escaped her ponytail. A fairly benign gesture, but it had the impact of an earthquake on his body. "You're asking me if I want to take you to bed."

That question had entered Michelle's mind on more than one occasion. So had the dangerous fantasy of him doing just that. "I don't mean to offend you, but I've had enough experience with other men—"

"I'm not other men." His voice was low and controlled, adamant. "But I'd be one helluva liar if I said the thought hadn't crossed my mind, because it has. In fact, if my daughter wasn't in the next room, and the prospect of Jared and Brooke's return wasn't hanging over us, I might be entertaining some of those thoughts. At least, at one time I might have.''

Michelle rubbed her bare arms, trying to rid herself of the sudden shakes. ''What do you mean 'at one time'?''

''A few months ago that was all that mattered to me. Just a quick roll and nothing more. But you've changed all that.''

''Me?''

''Yeah, you. I want to get to know you, Michelle. Outside of bed before we even consider getting in one together. I want to make love to you, you can bet on that. But only if and when we're ready. Until then, I'm content with mental foreplay.''

Mental foreplay? ''What is that supposed to mean?''

''It's that period of time when two people talk to each other in a way that sends a message loud and clear that they want each other. That old saying that sex begins with the mind is true. There's nothing wrong with fantasy until the time is right for the real thing. It's healthy and it's safe.''

Michelle drew in a deep breath and exhaled slowly. The lyrical sound of his voice, the seriousness in his expression, his fathomless midnight eyes, primed her racing pulse. ''I see. Then you prefer this mental foreplay to the real thing?''

''I'm not saying that. I'm saying it's all about timing. I got in a hurry once with a woman and it proved to be a huge mistake. I'm not going to make that mistake again.''

Her own bitter experience prompted her to ask, ''Before or after your divorce?''

His expression remained solemn. ''I didn't see any-

one until after my divorce, if that's what you're asking
me. I was faithful to my wife during my marriage, although she might argue that point.''

Michelle's eyebrow formed a question mark. ''She
accused you of fooling around?''

''Not with women. She claimed my job was my mis-
tress. And in a way she was right.''

She admired his honesty, if she could really believe
him. But she had to acknowledge he seemed less and
less like Brett. She also acknowledged that he was
drawing her in with his sensual words. Physically
drawing her closer. She rested one bent arm on the
counter and leaned into it for support. ''What about
chemistry between people, plain and simple?''

''That's important. It has to be there, but it shouldn't
be the only thing.''

Michelle felt as though someone had already lit a
Bunsen burner underneath her. ''So have you experienced some of this chemistry when you're around
me?''

''To the point of spontaneous combustion.''

He took a slow visual excursion down her body and
back up again. Although he stood a good ten inches
away, Michelle reacted as if he'd used his hands on
her in all the right places. Secret places.

Against her better judgment, she moved a little
closer and reached up to untie his bow tie, then tossed
it onto the counter like an experienced exotic dancer.

His eyes narrowed, but not before she caught a
glimpse of what she thought was desire. ''What are you
trying to do, Michelle? Drive me crazy?''

She slipped the top button on his collar. ''I'm trying
to make you more comfortable. You look a little uptight.''

"I am uptight, but it's not the tie."

She knew exactly what had him so ill at ease, but she had some primal need to hear him say it. "What's the problem, then?"

"You. I want to touch you. Put my hands on you. My mouth on you. Everywhere."

Her breasts tightened and heat pooled low in her belly, and lower, as if he had already done what he'd said he wanted to do. "What's stopping you?" She could not believe she'd asked that. She also couldn't believe that she actually wanted him to kiss her. *Needed* him to kiss her, as if he'd cast some sort of spell over her.

"First of all we're in your sister's kitchen," he said. "And then there's the fact that I've already decided we're going to take this nice and easy."

Usually that would be fine by Michelle, but Nick Kempner's sensuality made her feel anything but her usual self. Something was happening to her refined reserve. Something wild and inexplicable. She was about to do something totally crazy, totally out of character. A huge risk in light of her past experience with a man who'd only wanted one thing.

Leaning forward, Michelle let her eyes drift shut and braced for the impact of his lips on hers. Instead his hands grasped her shoulders and pushed her back.

"No way, Michelle. Not here. Not now."

Her eyes snapped open as if he'd slapped her in the face. "What's wrong with just a kiss?"

He dropped his hands and sidestepped away from her. "Because if I kiss you right now, I can't promise I'll stop."

That took some of the sting out of his rejection.

"And you think that I'd be so bowled over by your kiss that I wouldn't stop you?"

"I'm not willing to take that chance."

"What if I am?"

He sent her a cynical grin. "You're really making this hard on me. In every sense of the word."

Michelle felt a tad too devious. A bit too eager to see how long it took him to crumble. She strolled around the dinette and came to a stop immediately before him. "Oh, I get it. The doctor is all talk, and no action."

It took all of five seconds for Nick to span the space between them and answer Michelle's challenge, give her exactly what she wanted. She didn't have time to prepare for the urgent kiss, much less prepare for Nick raising her up and setting her down on the table's edge where he moved between her parted legs.

His lips were soft yet insistent, his tongue persuasive yet nonintrusive. He tasted like chocolate and mint, a flavor that set her senses on fire, as did his hands roving over her back, her rib cage, then up to frame her face as he deepened the kiss.

She managed to push his jacket away from his shoulders and at the same time thrust aside all the cautions swimming around in her brain. Only a natural disaster—or Nick—could derail the moment. Michelle didn't have the will or the want to.

No, nothing could stop this take-me-now kiss, at least from Michelle's standpoint. Except the sound of her sister's voice.

"What's that I smell brewing?"

Four

Trouble with a big fat T.

Nick spun away from the table—and Michelle—to face the cabinet before confronting Jared and Brooke. He braced his hands on the ledge and lowered his head. "Damn."

He only sensed Michelle's movement since he didn't dare look at her. He didn't dare turn around, either, until he'd recovered some semblance of his dignity. And worse, his jacket was somewhere on the floor. He couldn't even adequately hide his transgressions.

"Are we interrupting something?" This time Jared spoke, his tone more than a little suspicious.

Nick straightened and opened the cabinet nearest him. "Where'd you put all the coffee cups?"

Michelle was at his side once again, reaching around him to open another cabinet—brushing up against him, which didn't help his predicament one bit. "Right here," she said, fumbling for two mugs. Nick took two more and turned to meet Jared's I-caught-you expression.

Michelle held up the mugs. "Coffee anyone?"

Brooke appeared to be less skeptical than Jared, probably because she had more tact than her husband. "If I have coffee," she said, "I'll never get to sleep."

Neither would Nick, but caffeine wouldn't be the cause of his insomnia. His problem had to do with a region directly below the belt, thanks to Michelle's sudden loss of inhibition. He snatched his jacket from the floor, slipped it on and said, "On second thought, I believe I'll pass. I need to get Kelsey home."

"I need to go home, too," Michelle said, then hurried out into the hall, Brooke following behind.

Jared nodded toward the cabinet. "Forgetting something?"

Nick looked at his discarded bow tie suspended from the edge of the counter like a snake ready to strike. "Yeah. I hate that thing."

Before Nick could make a clean getaway, Jared blocked the entrance. "You know, pink's not really your shade."

It took a moment for the comment to register in Nick's short-circuited brain. He swiped a hand over his mouth and came back with a smudge of lipstick. He hadn't even noticed Michelle was wearing any. He doubted she had any left after that meltdown kiss. "I'm not in the mood for a lecture, Granger."

"I bet I know what you are in the mood for."

Nick elbowed his way past Jared and out into the hall, heading for his daughter and a quick getaway. Once in the den, he slipped his arms underneath Kelsey and held her close against his chest. She smelled like baby shampoo and innocence. If only he could keep her this way, untainted by the world and adult problems. God knew he had one problem to contend with—exactly what to do about Michelle Lewis.

Kelsey raised her head and studied him with a sleepy, unfocused gaze. "Wanna go home, Daddy."

"We are, sweetheart. Right now."

As he started for the door, he encountered Brooke and Jared waiting for his departure. *Great.* Judge and jury all rolled into one. But no Michelle. "Where'd your sister go?" Nick asked, trying to sound nonchalant and failing miserably.

"She rushed out, saying she needed to do some work," Brooke said.

"Yeah, she mentioned that." So much for saying good-night to Michelle. Nick shifted Kelsey to his shoulder. "'Night folks. Thanks."

Brooke held open the door for him. "Be sure to come back soon. I think Michelle really enjoyed the evening."

So had he. Too much. With a mumbled goodbye, Nick headed for his car, parked at the curb. As soon as he opened the rear door, Michelle emerged from the shadows of the nearby maple tree, taking him by surprise.

She stood by the hood of the car while Nick secured Kelsey into her booster seat. Thankfully his daughter continued to sleep during the process. At least maybe now he would have a few minutes to talk to Michelle.

He closed the door as quietly as possible and joined Michelle, who seemed to find the Bermuda grass beneath her feet much more fascinating than him.

"I won't keep you long," she said. "I only wanted to say I didn't mean for that to happen."

He tipped her chin up, forcing her to look at him. "Neither did I, but it did. So let's talk about it later. You look beat. You need to get some rest."

"Not *that* again."

"Sorry, but it's the doctor in me. I'm worried about you burning the candle at both ends. You need to take it easy before you make yourself sick."

"I'll try." She sounded too tired to argue.

Nick allowed some silence between them until he got a good grasp on what he wanted to say. "I was serious tonight when I told you I want us to get to know each other. I don't like the idea of playing games."

"Neither do I," she said defensively. And with less anger, added, "Not normally. But then I'm not normal around you."

"Is that a bad thing?"

"I haven't decided yet."

He offered her a smile in hopes of lightening the mood. "You seemed fine to me. Maybe a little impulsive, but I'll chalk that up to that old chemistry. Besides, I kind of enjoyed that side of you." All of his parts did.

She tried to smile, but it faltered. So did her gaze. "This thing between us—"

"Later, Michelle. We'll talk about it later." If he didn't get in his car and drive away, he would kiss her again and risk stirring his body back to life. As things now stood, literally, a night's sleep wouldn't even begin to remedy the problem.

She hugged her arms to her middle. "This probably isn't a good idea, what's happening between us. I don't think there's really anything more to say about it."

He rubbed a thumb over her lips, remembering.

Wanting. "Oh, yeah. I have plenty to say to you." And even more that he wanted to do with her.

Finally her smile came full force. "You're a stubborn man, Nick Kempner."

He took her slender hand into his. "One of my better traits." He winked. "If you give me a chance, I'll show you a few more."

With a smile she tugged her hand from his grasp, then turned and walked toward her car. Keeping her back to him, she said, "I can't wait."

Something in her tone told Nick that maybe she meant it.

When the knock came on her office door, Michelle nearly snapped her pencil in two. She wasn't ready to see Nick yet. Not after what had happened between them three days ago. Not after her reckless behavior and that kiss.

Oh, that kiss. That's all she had thought about on Sunday and yesterday at work. Just thinking about it now—and him—made her palms perspire, not to mention what it did to points unseen.

The door opened but not to Nick Kempner. Michelle didn't know whether she was relieved or disappointed. But she was happy to see Cassandra Allen, one of her few friends aside from Brooke.

Cassie entered the room like a whirlwind, as if she couldn't contain all her energy. "Can I bother you a sec?"

Michelle pushed back her chair and tossed the pencil aside. "Please. I could use the break."

Cassie slipped into the chair across from Michelle and finger combed her blond hair away from her face. "I wanted to stop by and say—" She froze midsentence and surveyed Michelle with keen brown eyes. "My gosh, you look horrible. Are you sick?"

Michelle pinched the bridge of her nose. If she heard that one more time, she would be forced to wear a bag over her head. "Yes, I'm sick. Sick to death of everyone telling me how bad I look." Did she have to sound so darned cranky?

"Sorry, but I imagine everyone's worried about you."

Michelle released a frustrated sigh. "No, I'm sorry. I'm also okay. Just a little tired, that's all."

Cassie leaned forward. "Are you sure that's all?"

"I'm sure. Now what were you about to say?"

"Only that I wanted to congratulate you on becoming an aunt soon. I've been out on vacation and I just now heard the news about Brooke."

Michelle wondered if she should talk to Cassie about her fears. After all, Cassie was a social worker. She dealt in comforting troubled souls. Not that Michelle was all that troubled. But since she couldn't very well voice her concerns to Brooke, Cassie would have to do. "I'm really worried about the pregnancy," Michelle said. "I'm worried about Brooke and the baby."

Cassie scooted the chair forward and folded her hands on the desk. "How so?"

"Brooke's asthma."

"I thought she had pretty much outgrown that."

"That's what she would like everyone to believe, but she still suffers attacks now and then."

"Does she have a good OB?"

"Sara Landers. The best."

"Then I'm sure everything will work out fine."

If only Michelle could believe that. "I also worry about the baby. What if she passes it on?"

Cassie shrugged. "I suppose that's a risk, but I've seen so much worse in the preemies whose parents I counsel. At least asthma is a manageable disease."

"Yeah, to a point. It manages to disrupt everyone's life."

From the look of guarded interest on Cassie's face, Michelle realized she had probably revealed too much.

Cassie sat back and folded her arms, assuming her professional persona. "Does this have something to do with how the asthma affected you as a sibling?"

The woman was too insightful, or perhaps Michelle was too obvious. "It's tough having an asthmatic child in the family. It's frightening to watch someone struggle to breathe. Everyone suffers at times because of it, especially the asthmatic."

"You mean *you* suffered because of it."

No, that wasn't it at all. Brooke had suffered, not Michelle. "It wasn't that big a problem for me, only bothersome at times, especially when Brooke was so sick. You spend so much time worrying, wondering what you can do—" Michelle frowned. "Gosh, I sound so selfish."

"No, it's not selfish. You have a right to be concerned."

"I'm worried about nothing. I'm sure everything will be fine." Michelle realized her assertion had probably sounded phony. She tried to hide the lies behind a smile.

"Have you thought about talking to Brooke about this? Tell her how you really feel to clear the air? You might feel better."

As far as Michelle was concerned, Brooke had been through enough living with the asthma and their mother's overprotectiveness. She deserved to be happy.

"Really, Cassie, I'm all right. I'm feeling much better already after talking to you. Thanks for letting me vent."

Cassie looked skeptical. "Okay. But if you want to talk, you know where to find me. Besides, we need to go out on the town one evening. I'm not seeing anyone right now. Are you?"

Michelle immediately thought about Nick. That certainly didn't qualify. They hadn't even been on a date. They had kissed, though.

Heaven help her, she couldn't get the man's lips off her mind. If only she had some sort of talisman to exorcise the image. "No, I'm not seeing anyone. Call me next week. This ad campaign should be winding down, and maybe I'll get a breather for a few days."

"Great. Got to get back to work now. I have a ton of case files to dispose of before the end of the day." Cassie stood and eyed Michelle once again. "Are you sure you're okay? You're awfully pale."

Probably because the office was incredibly warm, Michelle decided, thanks to thoughts of Nick Kempner. She could definitely use some water from the cooler. And a good nap. Since it was only a bit past noon, she would have to settle for the water. "I'm okay," she said as she stood. Then suddenly she realized she wasn't at all okay.

The room began to spin, shards of light splintered behind her eyes, and before she could prepare, the world went topsy-turvy, then dark.

"This wouldn't be the route I'd choose to get you flat on your back."

Forcing herself out of the surreal dream, Michelle's eyes fluttered open at the sound of the masculine voice.

A voice that was becoming all too familiar. And all too welcome.

She studied his face, the cleft of his chin, the worry in his dark eyes that he tried to disguise with a half smile.

Michelle looked around to gain her bearings. A sterile room with a curtained entry, the mattress underneath her small and unforgiving, the smells antiseptic and overpowering.

Glancing down, she suddenly realized her skirt was hiked up to her thighs, way past the point of decency. And Nick Kempner was playing witness to all her disheveled glory.

This certainly wasn't a dream. More like a nightmare.

She brought her hands to her face with some effort. Her limbs felt incredibly heavy. Her head was still foggy, but she remembered snippets of being rushed somewhere. "Mind if I ask what's going on here?"

She felt the mattress bend with his weight as he perched on the edge of the narrow bed. "You kind of passed out in your office. Some social worker caught you right after you got up close and personal with your desk."

Michelle dropped her hands to her sides. "Cassie caught me? That's impossible. She's six inches shorter than me."

"Obviously she managed. You might want to thank her next time you see her."

Nick rose and tossed a sheet over her legs. At least part of her dignity had been restored.

He again took his roost on the bed. "Do you remember what happened?"

Michelle strained her brain trying to recall the moments immediately before she lost consciousness. "I stood. The rest is fuzzy."

"You don't remember falling?"

"Not really." Right now her mind was a total blur, except for the fact she did remember that Nick was an orthopedic surgeon, not an E.R. doctor. "What are you doing here?"

"I happened to be right next door taking care of some guy who wiped out on a jet ski. Broken collarbone."

"Isn't there some E.R. person around who's supposed to handle me?"

"You don't like me handling you?"

Oh, yes. "I haven't noticed you doing anything yet."

He cleared his throat when a nurse breezed in, as if suddenly remembering he was supposed to be playing doctor in the literal sense. "Actually, I'm about to order some X rays of your ribs as soon as I examine you. Seems you hit the desk on the way down."

Michelle tried to sit up and encountered a shooting pain in her side. "Ouch!"

"Whoa. Just be still." Nick eased her back with one hand, then rose from the side of the bed. The nurse stood near the gurney while he began unbuttoning Michelle's blouse.

Michelle squeezed her eyes shut. Great. An audience. This was not what she had envisioned when she'd secretly imagined him undressing her. But he was simply being professional. And she was simply coming undone right along with the shirt.

Once he had the material parted, Nick palpated her sore rib cage. "That hurt?"

Yes, but mostly her pride. She forced her eyes open and spoke through gritted teeth. "Just a little."

"Sit up slowly and take a few deep breaths for me."

She complied while he listened to her chest with a stethoscope. "Okay, lie back down."

After she did, he pulled her blouse closed and said, "I don't think anything's broken, but you do have a nasty bruise coming up. At least it wasn't your head." He grinned. "You might've broken the desk."

Before Michelle could manage an appropriate comeback, Nick turned to the nurse and said, "Nancy, I want to order some labs," then he let go a litany of orders Michelle didn't understand.

Soon after, the woman came at her with an evil-looking needle attached to a tube, as well as a plastic holder with several other tubes. "Nancy's going to draw some blood," Nick said. "In the meantime, stay put until we can try to figure out why you fainted."

"I'm fine. I just got up too fast."

He moved to one side to allow the nurse/vampire access to her arm. "That could be, but you're not going anywhere until we make sure."

Nick turned to the counter and started making notes. The nurse slapped a rubber tourniquet around Michelle's arm and drew blood while Michelle glared at Nick's back. She couldn't imagine that all this fuss was actually necessary. For goodness' sake, she'd only fainted. More than likely she had fallen asleep on her feet.

Once Nancy Nurse was done and out the door, Nick faced Michelle and leaned back against the counter. "One more question. Is there any chance you might be pregnant?"

How much more humiliation could she be subjected

to in one day? "You have to be exposed first," she muttered.

"Is that a no?"

"Yes. I mean no, there's absolutely no chance I could be pregnant. Unless it's the longest pregnancy in history—three years to be exact."

"Three years, huh?" His expression held the cast of satisfaction.

Michelle regretted making that admission. "Yes, is that a problem? I personally don't believe celibacy leads to fainting." Having Nick alleviate her of that problem might.

Nick grinned as if he'd read her murky mind. "Take it easy for a while, and I'll be back after I write the orders for your X rays."

"Is that really necessary?"

He winked. "Yeah. So don't go anywhere."

With that he was gone.

Michelle closed her eyes again, wishing she could go to sleep and wake to find this wasn't real. Wishing she was home in her bed…with Nick. The man was a sexy pest who wouldn't go away. Even as Michelle drifted off to sleep, he was the last image in her mind….

The curtain slid open, thrusting Michelle out of the pleasant haze of sleep.

"Are you all right, Michelle?"

Michelle opened her eyes to Cassie. "Yeah. Thanks for saving me from the nosedive."

"I wish I could've caught you before you hit your side on the edge of your desk. Do they think you've broken any ribs?"

"Probably not. But Dr. Kempner's ordering an X ray."

"Nick Kempner?" Cassie fanned her face. "Now he's worth a broken bone or two."

If Cassie only knew. Maybe she did know. Maybe she'd dated Nick. Of course not, Michelle thought. Nick had called her "some social worker." Besides, Cassie would have told her that. Heck, the whole hospital would have known.

The curtain parted once again "Shelly, are you okay?"

Brooke stood beside Cassie, hovering over Michelle like a mama helicopter.

Had someone notified the local media? "What are you doing here, Brooke? You should be home taking it easy."

"This is only temporary, and my well-being is not the issue at the moment. I'm more concerned about you."

Good grief. "Stop looking like I'm on my last leg, Brooke. I'm okay. Honest. I just got up too fast and fainted. People do it all the time."

"I'm sure that's all it is," Brooke said, "but it's better if you get checked out. I ran into Nick outside. Seems he has everything under control."

Oh, he had everything under control all right, except for Michelle's pounding heart. She had tried not to think of him as anything but a doctor when he had his hands on her ribs, but he wasn't your average doctor. Certainly better looking than most. Not that he'd done anything the least bit unprofessional. She'd noticed he had avoided looking at her bra, except for maybe a split second. Then again, she was probably imagining things.

Brooke and Cassie exchanged hellos, congratulations and thanks, as if they were all at a tea party.

"What's up with my sister-in-law?"

Jared breezed into the room and immediately picked up her chart. Heavens to Betsy, were they selling tickets outside?

Come one, come all, see the hospital's gorked public relations coordinator laid out on the table like a slab of meat.

"Hi, Jared," Michelle said with a friendliness she didn't exactly feel, in deference to her sister. "Please tell me I don't need a cardiac consultation."

Jared slapped the chart closed, walked to Brooke and rested his hands on her shoulders. "Not yet. We'll have to see what your labs say."

Rolling her eyes took too much energy, but Michelle managed it, anyway. "I think everyone's making a big deal out of this. So I fainted? I have a bruise on my ribs, otherwise I'm fine."

"She didn't look fine before she fainted," Cassie allowed. "She was very pale."

So much for good friends.

Brooke narrowed her eyes into a serious glare. "You have been a mother hen to me for years, Michelle Lewis, and now it's my turn. You will remain in that bed and behave yourself until you have a thorough examination. You won't get up until you receive a clean bill of health. Is that understood?"

"You better listen to her, Michelle," Jared said. "She can be one mean sister if you don't do what she says. Believe me, I know."

"I'm so scared," Michelle said with a good heaping of sarcasm.

Brooke continued to scowl even though her smile threatened to appear. "You should be afraid of me. Very afraid."

"Well, I better go," Cassie said as she headed toward the door. "Take care, Michelle. I'll check on you later."

"I need to go, too," Jared said. "I have a case in fifteen minutes." He bent and kissed Brooke smack on the lips, much longer than Michelle cared to witness.

Michelle released an impatient sigh. "If you two are going to make out, would you do it in the hall? I'd like to take a nap since I'm obviously stuck here for a while."

Jared and Brooke smiled in unison. "Sorry," Brooke said. "I haven't seen him since this morning."

"How appalling." More sarcasm Michelle couldn't contain. For some reason she felt even crankier now. No one had ever kissed her like that in public. Not that she would ever allow it. At least, she didn't think so, unless of course it involved...

"Okay, I'm back."

Obviously, Nick Kempner had developed telepathic powers, at least where Michelle's devious thoughts were concerned.

He strolled into the room holding several pieces of paper. Jared looked over Nick's shoulder, Brooke at his side. A few yeahs and uh-huhs broke through the momentary silence.

Michelle lifted her head and stared at the trio. "Do you mind sharing with me?"

Nick approached the bed first. "Your labs look fairly normal. Your potassium's a little low. When did you last eat?"

Michelle had to think on that one. "Lunch."

"What did you eat?"

"The same thing I had for breakfast."

"And what was that?"

"Coffee."

"Michelle Lewis!" Brooke propped a hand on her hip and looked as stern as a headmaster. "You've always been such a health nut. What were you thinking?"

"I haven't had time to think." Not exactly the truth. She'd been thinking about Nick Kempner, and often. "I've been busy with work, Mom and Dad, the usual stuff."

"Considering the hours she's keeping," Nick added, "she's probably fatigued on top of a poor diet."

"You're right on that count," Jared said. "She's a regular PR machine."

Nick rubbed his chin. "She could probably use some time off and a steady diet. To be on the safe side, I'll call in an internist and have him do a full work-up."

Michelle had just lost the last of her patience. "Would you guys stop talking like I'm not here! This is my health, and I think I should have some say in the matter."

Nick laid a hand on her arm. "Calm down. This is for your own good. We need to rule out all the possibilities."

Brooke leaned down and hugged Michelle's neck. "We'll leave you in Nick's capable hands for now." She turned to Nick. "And do whatever you have to do to keep her in that bed."

The man actually grinned. "My pleasure."

Brooke sent Michelle a warning frown. "Mind your manners, Shelly. I'll call you at home this evening."

"If they ever let me out of here," Michelle mumbled.

Brooke and Jared left, but Nick didn't. He reclaimed his place on the edge of the bed and took her hand.

"If everything checks out okay, then I have a proposition to make."

Michelle snickered in an attempt to ignore the steady flow of chills playing up and down her spine over Nick's touch. "I think this bed's a little too small for that, Doctor."

A wily grin spread across his face. "You're right. Not enough room. I have to admit, though, it might be worth a try."

No kidding, Michelle thought.

"But that's not what I was going to propose," he said.

"What, then?"

"You need to take a few days off. Get some rest."

She yanked her hand out of his grasp. "It's the middle of the week. I promised to help Mom plan Brooke's baby shower. Not to mention I still have work—"

"All that can wait. I'll clear it with the powers that be for you to take some time off. Doctor's orders."

Michelle fisted her hands at her sides and spoke through clenched teeth. "How noble of you. I can't tell you how much I appreciate your concern. You can't imagine how much I love the thought of being a prisoner in my own home."

"Not your home. My home."

Surely he wasn't serious. "I don't need a nursemaid."

"You do need to get away from this place. And I have the perfect solution."

"And that includes me moving in with you?"

"Temporarily. And not in town. I have a house in Marble Falls on the lake. It's a small A-frame, fairly secluded, but there's plenty of room for you and me."

The Alamodome wouldn't be big enough for the

both of them, at least where his hard-to-ignore sensuality and Michelle's out-of-control libido were concerned. "I think that's a dangerous idea, Dr. Kempner."

"It's a great idea. You'll have your own room. You'll have me at your beck and call. I'll be the perfect gentleman. All I expect from you is your company and your cooperation where your diet is concerned. The rest we'll play by ear."

Michelle really liked the idea of playing with Nick at the lake. She slapped the treacherous thoughts from her brain before she did something stupid, like agree to go. "It would be best if I stayed at home, in case someone needs me."

"That's exactly why you don't need to stay at home. My place has an unlisted number. No one can reach you there except Brooke and Jared, and your mother if you'd like."

"Heavens, no. Don't tell her. She'll have a fit."

"Then you'll come?"

Michelle bit her bottom lip. "I don't know—"

"Think about it, okay?" He stood again and sent her another heart-stopping grin. Thank goodness she was in the E.R. in case her own pump quit pumping.

"In the meantime," he said, "they'll take you up for your X rays, and I'll call in an internal medicine consult. I'll make sure they get it done, ASAP. Hopefully you'll be out of here in an hour or two. That should give you plenty of time to get a good night's sleep. I have to work until noon, but I'm off on Thursdays. I'll have my staff rearrange my schedule for the rest of the week. That way we'll have tomorrow afternoon through Sunday, since this isn't my weekend with Kelsey."

He said the last sentence with a hint of sadness and regret. Obviously, he missed not having that time with his daughter. But that wasn't the point. Right now he wanted Michelle to commit to filling his weekend hours. Was she a replacement for Kelsey, or did he really want her company? Spending time with Nick wasn't such a dreadful prospect. Still, she needed to think about it.

Michelle gave him her best scowl, but it obviously wasn't effective enough because he smiled. "You have it all planned out, don't you?" she asked.

"Yeah. All you have to do is say yes."

She wasn't falling for that one again. "I'll consider your proposition. But you might want to hold off rearranging your life for me until I decide. I don't want to inconvenience you."

He took her hand and brought it to his lips for a gentle kiss. "Michelle, I don't see this as an inconvenience. I see it as an opportunity. One I don't think either of us wants to miss. I don't expect anything from you except companionship. That and a promise you'll try to relax."

Could she really relax around him? Did she have the nerve to agree to spend that much time with him? Did she really believe for one minute that they could share a remote house and do nothing more than talk?

Probably not, but she would take tonight and pretend to think it over…then politely tell him no tomorrow.

Five

Nick couldn't believe that Michelle had said yes, but she had, and now they were on their way to the lake.

Luckily, she'd received a clean bill of health the day before. Her fainting had been the result of a poor diet and exhaustion, doing too much for too many and not enough for herself. Nick had expected that diagnosis. Had hoped for it, even. When he'd seen her being wheeled into the E.R. on a gurney, he'd felt nothing less than blind panic. He honestly couldn't stand the thought of anything happening to Michelle.

That thought made him pause and reassess where this thing between them was heading and how far he wanted it to go. Now Thursday, he had all of four days to see if Michelle was even willing to consider more than a few days together. If that's what *he* really wanted.

As he turned onto the rural farm-to-market road

leading to the house, he glanced at Michelle, who continued to sleep, as she had been doing most of the three-hour trip. She looked totally relaxed, her face slack and content. Good. She needed to sleep. And Nick would be smart to remember that.

He kept coming back to her revelation in the E.R. She hadn't been with a man in three years. Obviously she *had* sworn off men, which made Nick all the more proud that she'd agreed to come with him, and all the more determined not to scare her off by pushing too hard or too fast. He would make it his goal to prove that she hadn't made a mistake. He also vowed to maintain control over his baser urges.

But man, oh, man, if she kissed him again the way she had the other night at Jared's, he couldn't promise he would refuse her anything. He'd almost lost it that night. Two more minutes and the Grangers might have seen a lot more than they'd bargained for, namely his pants around his ankles and his hands on Michelle in places that shouldn't be explored outside a bedroom, much less in a kitchen. Unless they were guaranteed privacy.

Nick mentally groaned and reprimanded himself for letting his imagination get totally out of hand once again, at his body's expense. He needed to back off in order to prove his honor, at least in her eyes. Prove to her that he wasn't just some man on the make determined to take advantage of an exhausted woman. He wouldn't mind at all, though, if she did decide to take advantage of him.

Cut it out, Nick.

This could very well be the hardest weekend he had ever spent with a woman. Achingly hard. In every sense of the word.

When he hit the rutted road leading up to the cabin, Michelle came awake with a start. She pushed her long hair from her face and straightened, but still looked disoriented. "Are we here?" she asked, her voice hoarse with sleep.

"Yeah. Almost." Nick pointed ahead. "It's right there on that hill."

She stared out the windshield, squinting against the August sun until they passed under the overhang of trees lining the drive. The cedar cabin sat shaded by a thick stand of oak and ash, trees Nick had insisted they save when he'd had the place built six years ago. Kids needed trees, and in a few months he planned to build a treetop fort for his daughter. A special place for dad and daughter, before Kelsey got too old and preferred the mall and boys to his company.

For a moment Nick immersed himself in melancholy memories, recollections of the few good times spent here before the divorce, when they'd all seemed happy—him, Bridget and the baby. Before things got ugly and the idea of continuing on as a real family had become only an illusion. Before all the accusations, the suspicions, the angry, hurtful words. Before it was too late to go back and pick up the pieces.

When the house came into full view, Michelle's sharp indrawn gasp drew his attention. Her mouth dropped open. "My gosh, Nick. That's not small. I could put my whole apartment on the deck. It's absolutely breathtaking."

He glanced at the approaching cabin and suddenly realized he'd taken for granted the way the house stood majestic against the rustic backdrop. But he remembered having those same feelings of awe right after it had been built. Nice that he could now enjoy the place through Michelle's eyes. "The floor-to-ceiling glass windows make it look bigger than it really is."

She glanced at him with a skeptical smile. "Obviously, you didn't get a good look at my apartment when you picked me up."

No, he hadn't. He'd scarcely gotten in the door before she'd practically shoved him back out. He planned to get a better look one of these days.

Pulling into the drive, he'd barely cut the engine before Michelle flew out the passenger door. While she walked the perimeter of the front yard, Nick opened the sedan's trunk and withdrew her bags. He stopped on his way to the house to watch her. She paused at the swing he'd built for Kelsey and ran a hand down the rope with a gentle caress. Slipping onto the flat wooden seat, she began to swing back and forth, at first slowly, then faster and faster with childlike abandon.

Her gleaming dark hair flowed behind her, her face aglow as a smile tipped the corners of her mouth. Her long legs showing from beneath the khaki shorts shot out in front of her as she pumped to gain altitude. Her full breasts, outlined by navy knit, thrust forward with her efforts and made Nick's heart pound at an alarming rate.

Nick set the two bags on the bottom steps leading to the front door to take in the view. He wished he'd brought his camera to capture the moment—Michelle Lewis, the consummate professional woman, on a kid's swing with the most joyful look on her face that Nick had ever seen on any adult.

As ridiculous as it seemed, he was jealous of the damned swing. If only she would look that way when she was with him. Maybe someday she would. Maybe even before they left here. If he played his cards right.

Michelle let the swing drift to a stop and laughed. "Gosh, that was great!"

Yeah, a real fine moment, in Nick's opinion. He found he liked her throaty laugh as much as he liked everything else about her. "Glad you enjoyed it. You care to join me in the house now?"

She shrugged. "I guess. Can we swing later?"

If he had his way they would, inside, outside, didn't matter to him.

Jeez, he needed to get a grip, and not necessarily on Michelle. Not yet. "Sure, we can do anything you want after dinner. But first you need to eat. It's getting late."

"Spoilsport." She stuck out her lip in a pretend pout and strolled up to him.

When she tried to take her bag from him, he wouldn't let her. "I've got it. You don't need to exert yourself."

She crossed her arms under her breasts. "You're a regular little taskmaster, aren't you?"

"Yeah, and don't forget it. I'd hate to have to get out my whips and chains so you'll do my bidding."

"Now that sounds really kinky." She raised a brow and grinned. "And interesting."

"Get up the stairs, Michelle, before I—"

"Before you what?"

Kiss the life out of you. "Before I get a hernia."

"Okay." With that she bounded up the steep redwood stairs, leaving Nick behind to enjoy the view. And what a view it was—a flash of thigh as her shorts tightened with every step, her narrow waist, her great butt that made Nick's hands itch to grab a handful and never let go.

Nick followed behind, slowly, just so he could look

his fill. It would take a major effort on his part not to try to touch his fill.

Michelle couldn't believe she'd agreed to come, but after considering the offer, and Brooke's advice, she'd decided to take the chance, tired of living by standards that no longer held any appeal. She was determined to have some fun with Nick while keeping her emotions in check. That she could do. After all, it was only a long weekend.

She also couldn't believe that Nick had been so blasé about the house. She stood inside the great room, admiring the massive wall-length stone fireplace sporting a gigantic hearth, the rustic earth-toned, Southwest-patterned furniture set out randomly around the room, the huge woven rug covering the hardwood floor, complementing the decor. If this was Nick's idea of simple, then she couldn't imagine what he thought of her cracker-box apartment.

She turned to find him staring at her, the bags at his feet. He gestured to the staircase to his left. "You'll be staying up there. It's an open loft. You can look over the railing down to this room. There's a full bath upstairs, and a half bath down here."

Michelle glanced up the stairway, then back at him. "Where's your room?"

He pointed at the sofa positioned in front of the windows. "Right there."

She frowned. "Nick, that's totally unfair. You shouldn't have to sleep on a couch."

"I've slept on it before."

She wondered if that was due to an argument with his ex, or by his own choice. She certainly didn't intend to ask. "Are you sure? I have no problem sleeping there. I spent a good deal of time on the sofa before Brooke moved out of the apartment and in with Jared."

He scooped up her bags and started up the stairs. "No way. You're my guest, so you get the best accommodations."

Michelle followed him up the stairs, admiring the pull of muscles in his bare calves, the way his white shorts set off his tanned, well-formed thighs. And oh, what a wonderful bottom. She had the strongest urge to reach up and give one cheek a pinch. Just a little pinch. In slow motion her hand headed straight for the intended target....

"I'll have to use the shower up here since there's not one downstairs," he said over one shoulder.

Michelle snatched her hand back, thankful she hadn't gotten caught. What in the heck was wrong with her? Perhaps she *had* hit her head yesterday.

"Oh, I thought you might bathe in the lake," she teased.

Nick stopped at the top landing, dropped the bags, then leaned forward with hands braced on the railing. He was much too close for any semblance of comfort. "Why, Michelle Lewis, are you suggesting I skinny-dip?" He drawled his words like he had the day she'd encountered him in the hospital hallway.

The man was just too charming for his own good. "Only if you have a pair of binoculars so I can watch."

"Oh, so you're into that?"

She hadn't been into *anything* until she'd met him. "Maybe. By the way, where is the lake?"

Nick left the landing, allowing her passage to join him in the loft, giving her space to breathe and time to recover from his close proximity.

The bedroom was as rustic as the living area, one

paneled wall flanked by a heavy oak sleigh bed covered in a navy-blue down comforter. Muted light filtering in from the evening sun crossed the bed in ribbons. The area smelled of rich cedar and invigorating cologne. Masculine, sensual, like the man.

He set her bags on the cedar chest at the end of the bed and signaled her to join him at the railing. "The lake's right over there."

She came to his side and stared out the tinted windows spanning the front of the great room. Just beyond the tree line, Michelle caught a glimpse of blue water and the now setting sun. The scene was something out of a painting, a mix of oranges and pinks and baby blues.

"This is an incredible view," she said wistfully.

"Yeah, it is."

She glanced at Nick to find he wasn't looking out the windows at all. He was looking right at her with a smile that could dissolve the rubber soles on her sneakers. Her gaze drifted away as she resisted the urge to push the lock of dark hair falling across his forehead. Resist his intense eyes and his smile that could wither the most stoic woman's resolve. Resist kissing him once again with a bed at their back and no threat of unwelcome guests to interrupt.

Michelle slapped her palms on the railing and the crazy ideas from her head. "Well, I have to admit I'm famished." Hungry for Nick's touch much more than food.

Maybe she would have him for dessert. Maybe she should harness her hormones before she did something unwise, like tackle him downstairs and make good use of the rug in front of the fireplace.

"Okay."

Had she inadvertently said that? "Okay what?"

"Okay, you unpack while I fix dinner."

"I'm not helpless. In fact, I really enjoy cooking. I can give you a hand with whatever you need."

He slipped his hands in the pocket of his shorts as if he needed to control them. "You know, Michelle. You really should think about these offers you keep making. One day I'm going to take you up on them."

"One day I might let you." Michelle couldn't believe she'd said that. Nick was the one with all the sexy innuendo and bedroom lines. Could someone become a flirt by osmosis?

"Promises, promises," he said with a grin.

Trying to look serious, she straightened the collar on his shirt and patted his chest. "Let's get one thing straight, Dr. Kempner. I'm a woman of my word."

Now he looked all too serious. "I know that. And like I told you from the beginning, the time we have together is for you to relax and us to get to know each other."

She smiled. "That's exactly what we should do. Get to know each other." She would simply have to decide how well.

Nick's body was hotter than the flame under the skillet. He raked the stir-fry vegetables from the cutting board into the pan, causing the oil to sizzle, just like the blood in his veins.

He took a step back and braced his hands on the counter, head down to study the tile floor, much the same as he had in the Grangers' kitchen the other night.

He damn sure needed to quit thinking about that, among other things. But every word Michelle uttered had kept his muscles clenching for control and his body ignoring the effort.

Man, he wished he were stronger. He wished it hadn't been so long since he'd been with a woman. Not that being with someone else before Michelle would really matter. Deep down he knew he would still want her. But he honestly did need to know what lurked beneath all that cool reserve before he explored other possibilities—a totally untried notion for him and one that he welcomed. He had made so many mistakes with Bridget, the least of which had to do with marrying her because it had seemed like the right thing at the time. The expected thing. He'd had a burgeoning career, so why not a wife?

That didn't mean he hadn't loved Bridget in his own way. It did mean that he hadn't really known her. They were good together in bed, and he knew all too well that unbridled passion sometimes muddled the real issues, like compatibility outside the realm of great sex. He was anything but compatible with Bridget, yet neither of them had realized that before it had been too late. Before they'd set off into the uncharted territory of holy wedlock.

"What's got you so deep in thought?"

Nick straightened and turned from the stove to see Michelle plop down into an oak barrel chair. She'd changed into a white oversize T-shirt that hung off one shoulder and ragged cutoffs, her hair piled up on her head, bare feet revealing neatly painted red toenails. The woman even had sexy feet.

"Just thinking about what we're going to do tomorrow," he said. And tonight.

"And what do you have planned for the rest of the week?" she asked with a casual smile.

That was a loaded question. He planned to keep his distance, but seeing her sitting there looking totally at home in what once had been Bridget's kitchen, looking like a man's finest fantasy and a woman's greatest nemesis, shot all his plans straight to hell and back.

He turned to the stove, away from Michelle's sensual aura and sultry smile. "I thought we'd take the boat out tomorrow morning. Have lunch onboard." He glanced back at her. "Do you like to fish?"

"I never have before, so I don't know."

"Your dad never took you fishing?"

"Oh, he would've liked to, but Mom would have none of that."

"Why not?"

"Well, Brooke, mainly. We didn't spend a lot of time outdoors because of her allergies. And it wouldn't have been fair to her if I got to go and she didn't."

Things were beginning to become all too clear to Nick. No wonder she had enjoyed the swing. He would guess that she hadn't spent much of her childhood doing the normal things kids do because of Brooke's asthma, thanks to her strong sense of fair play. He admired that about Michelle, her obvious sense of selflessness, but he wondered if she had suffered because of it.

He reclined against the stove and shoved his hands into his pockets. "So you missed out on a lot back then, huh?"

"Brooke and I managed. We had very good imaginations. I didn't mind at all." The hesitation in her tone said otherwise, and he couldn't really blame her.

Nick went back to the skillet and stirred the vegetables with a vengeance, his mind switching into overdrive. Michelle had probably been thrust into the role of caregiver way too soon, exactly why she was so good with kids, namely Kelsey. She'd probably had to grow up fast. And she would probably still continue to take care of the entire family, especially now that Brooke and Jared had a baby on the way.

His thoughts shut off when he realized Michelle was now standing behind him, smelling better than the food. Right behind him, attempting to peer over his shoulder. When she wasn't successful, she propped her hands on his waist and leaned around him. Her breasts grazed his back. He started to sweat.

"Hope you like chicken," he said, adding the meat to the mix, running on autopilot since he couldn't rely on rational thought with her so close.

"Chicken's fine. I do try to avoid red meat, though."

"So much for the steaks I planned to cook tomorrow." So much for keeping his distance with Michelle's breasts at his back and her breath fanning the side of his neck. If she didn't stop rubbing against him, he'd be able to stir the veggies without the benefit of a spoon.

"I don't mind indulging now and then," she said. Her voice had a breathless quality about it, which complemented the sudden lack of oxygen in Nick's lungs that seemed to refuse to inflate. Unfortunately, another part of his body was definitely inflating.

Down, boy.

"Great. We'll have steaks tomorrow night." He covered the skillet with a lid. "I'll just let this simmer a few minutes." He was already simmering low in his gut, knowing it was only a matter of time before he would reach the boiling point if he didn't get away from her.

Turning, he realized she hadn't moved an inch.

Maybe an inch, but toward him, not away from him. He curled his hands around her trim waist, intending to set her aside. But that wasn't what his brain—or his body—intended at all.

She draped her arms around his neck, and the next move he executed came solely from instinct. He kissed her, even though in the back of his mind he realized he probably shouldn't. But he couldn't help it. His recent discovery that kissing Michelle Lewis was just this side of heaven prevented him from pulling away, even though he'd have hell trying to stop.

She was pliant in his arms and tasted like mint, but the effect she was having on him went straight to his head, like a double scotch. She played on his weakness with a few strokes of her tongue, sending his body into orbit and his hands into action. He nudged her hips forward and stroked his fingertips up and down over the curve of her bottom, the way he'd wanted to do when he'd watched her take the stairs.

She leaned farther into him. The heat coming from the flame at his back was nothing compared to the inferno building below his belt. That fire caused him to forget his well-laid plans and all his determination not to rush into anything. He couldn't ignore her breasts pressed against his chest or his pulse pounding away in his ears, or the fact he had the mother of all erections. And he couldn't ignore the way her hips began to move in a rhythm that was about to drive him totally insane.

He pulled the shirt from her shorts and slipped his hand up her bare back. It wasn't enough. He slid his fingertips around her side—and contacted her ribs. When she flinched, the carnal fog began to clear.

He remembered why they had come here in the first

place. Michelle needed to rest and relax, and she couldn't do that if he put her through the workout his body now demanded, a workout that involved taking off a minimal amount of clothing and utilizing the kitchen table so he could bury himself inside her until they didn't give a damn about the stir-fry.

He dropped his hands and broke the kiss, then set her aside, as he should have done in the first place. "If we don't stop, I'm going to burn your dinner."

"You're right." She sounded winded and looked wonderful, with her swollen lips and eyes clouded with desire. But she didn't look all that happy, and that's what he wanted to see—the pure joy plastered across her face that had appeared when she'd been on the swing.

He flipped the burner off from under the stove. "Maybe we should set some ground rules before things get too out of hand."

She reclaimed her seat at the dinette, but this time her frame seemed stiff. "You don't strike me as the type of person who lives by many rules."

That made him almost angry. "I do when I have to."

"That's all I've done, and I'm really getting tired of it."

He understood what she meant, but that didn't change what he knew to be true. Passion could screw up the prospect of a meaningful relationship. "Look, Michelle, I told you I don't want to play games. I think we need to slow down, take it easy." The words were totally foreign to his mouth, but somehow they didn't feel that way where Michelle was concerned.

"Nick, it was just a kiss. And if you recall, the second kiss." She looked around the room. "What is it about kissing in a kitchen? I've never even done that before you.''

For a moment he wondered exactly what she had done before him. She sure as heck didn't kiss like a novice. In reality, he didn't want to know. Just thinking about Michelle with another man, another lover—in a kitchen or elsewhere—made him mad. ''Maybe the appeal of a kitchen has something to do with what's cooking between us.'' A really lame pun.

Michelle obviously thought so, too. She rolled her eyes to the ceiling, then slapped her palms on her thighs and stood. ''Okay, I think we should keep our lips to ourselves. If you insist.''

No, he didn't insist. At least his body didn't. ''We'll see what happens, okay?''

''Okay. We'll see what happens,'' she said, sounding as if she knew exactly what was going to happen. So did he.

Nick didn't figure keeping the hands-off vow would come easily for either one of them. They could try, at least for today. Tomorrow was another thing altogether. ''Okay. We'll just have to restrain ourselves.''

But Nick knew that restraint would only come if Michelle either stayed completely away from him or shackled him.

He set plates full of the stir-fry on the table while Michelle sat in silence, focused on some unknown point across the room. He wondered what she was thinking. Did she believe that coming here with him was a mistake? Did she wish she were somewhere else? If so, he intended to change her mind. And he would do that by keeping his fly zipped along with his mouth, at least for the time being.

They ate while engaging in mindless chatter and

more than a few laughs: Nick shared some off-color medical jokes, Michelle filled him in on some of the latest administrative office gossip with special asides about the main players. They discovered they had the same taste in music, a mutual love of the great outdoors and a passion for their careers. They agreed on many social issues and discussed their respective families—Nick's sisters, Kelsey, Michelle's overprotective mother and doting dad. Family was truly important to them both.

Nick was beginning to make some surprising observations. They had a lot in common, more than he'd ever believed. But more important, Michelle made him feel happy to be alive, made him want her even more.

Despite what they'd learned about each other, Nick wanted to know all her secrets. He was totally captive to the mysteries still hiding behind Michelle's beautiful smile and crystal-blue eyes. He had a strong feeling there was no escaping her charms. Not that he really wanted to.

Once the conversation lulled and they settled into comfortable quiet, Michelle pushed back her chair and rubbed her belly. "That was great, but I think I ate too much."

Nick followed the innocent movement of her hand on her abdomen, thinking less than innocent thoughts. He couldn't help but imagine his own hand there, and elsewhere. "Hope you left room for dessert."

"What did you have in mind?"

Nothing appropriate. "Strawberries and cream."

"First I want to take a shower," she said. "Is that okay with you?"

Nick picked up the plates and put them in the sink, trying really hard not to imagine Michelle in the shower. But when he turned the water on, that's exactly what he imagined. "No problem. Take your time."

She rose and walked to the sink to stand beside him. "Why don't you let me clean this mess? I feel so useless."

He shot her a glance. "Nope. I'm your slave for the night. Take advantage of my hospitality while you can. Tomorrow I might make you chop wood."

"And maybe catch a rabbit or two for the barbecue?"

He laughed. "No way. Kelsey would never forgive me if I fried Peter Cottontail."

"Can't say that I blame her."

The sudden quiet was interrupted only by the sound of water running in the sink, until Michelle finally spoke again. "Nick, I just wanted to say that I really appreciate everything. I'm glad I came."

Nick couldn't have been more pleased if she'd told him he'd won the Nobel Prize for innovations in orthopedic surgery. "I'm glad, too. Now take your shower and then join me on the sofa."

"You're already planning to take me to your bed?"

He frowned. "Get out of here, Michelle Lewis, before I'm tempted to take a bath with you." He tried to sound like he was kidding, but in reality he'd like nothing better.

She winked. "We'll save that for later. In the lake."

Spinning on her bare feet, she swayed out of the kitchen, sparing Nick another spontaneous kiss. If she even so much as looked as if she might touch him, he would probably come totally untrained.

Fortunately, it was a big couch.

Six

If the sofa happened to be a mile long, enough space wouldn't exist to prevent Michelle's overwhelming need to jump the orthopedic surgeon's fabulous bones.

But at the moment she was curled up on one end of the couch with her legs beneath her; Nick was on the other end with his long legs propped on the coffee table before them. At least she could try to control herself, unlike her lack of control earlier that evening.

Maybe he was right. Maybe things were moving too fast. But every time he kissed her, she became helpless putty in his hands. She had no will to fight him, and if he didn't have that steely resolve, he could have had his way with her in the kitchen, or anywhere for that matter. Even on the sofa where they now sat.

Michelle brushed her damp hair out of her face and picked up her glass of wine. Perhaps if she guzzled it she might forget her devilish thoughts. Or act on them.

She gave her attention to the scene outside to avoid looking at him. "I didn't think anything would top seeing the sun setting, but that was before all the stars came out."

"Yeah. Kelsey and I like to sit here and try to count them. She usually falls asleep before we get to twenty."

The image of Nick counting stars with his daughter blanketed Michelle's heart with warmth and true admiration. Brooke had been right. He was a good dad. A good man. On first impression, Michelle would never have believed that about him. She'd viewed him as a primo playboy, interested only in the next conquest, another notch on his scalpel, not at all unlike another man she'd known. A man who had colored her judgment for years.

Now she was beginning to realize that Nick's charm was something that came naturally to him. An aspect of his personality that he couldn't control. It didn't make him evil or totally unredeemable in Michelle's eyes. It did make her more cautious.

Yet the warm, fuzzy feelings surfacing for Nick overrode her concerns and drew Michelle close to his side, probably at the risk of his rejection. Still, she craved the contact, his warmth, something she hadn't had in a very long time.

She tried to curl up beside him but he leaned forward and picked up a strawberry. Surprisingly he sat back and draped his free arm over the back of the sofa, allowing her the contact she so desperately needed from him.

"Here. Have a berry." He touched the fruit to her lips.

She took it and chewed but found it difficult to swallow. She finally did, with effort. "It's good."

"Then you do like fruit."

"Yes. Why?"

"I don't know. Just something Jared told me. He said that if you're anything like Brooke, I should bring along a lot of fruit."

Michelle frowned. "I have no idea what he's talking about."

"Neither do I, but I have a feeling it's pretty personal."

Michelle couldn't imagine Brooke doing something suggestive with fruit. But then, she hadn't imagined Brooke falling in love again when she'd seemed so adamant not to. And now she was having a baby.

The concern for her sister came calling once more, but she pushed it away. "Maybe some day I'll ask Brooke about it."

Leaning forward, Michelle scooped up a handful of strawberries and popped one into Nick's mouth.

His smile surfaced, revealing perfect teeth accentuated by the dark shading of whiskers on his jaw. "We've been here less than a day and we're already feeding each other berries. Pretty romantic for a rogue like me, huh? Who would've thought it?"

Certainly not Michelle. Romantic gestures were something she hadn't discovered in most men's dating repertoire, except for one man. But he had used the technique as a means to an end, a method to get what he'd wanted from her. Which led Michelle to tell Nick something she never dreamed she would reveal, at least not now. But she felt the need to explain, to make him understand why being with him was such a huge step for her. Let him know up-front what a fool she could be when it came to relationships.

"I've only had one lover, Nick."

His smile faded. "We don't have to talk about that, Michelle. What happened in your past doesn't matter to me, at least where we're concerned."

But it did matter to Michelle, the reason why she chose to continue. "He was married."

Anger sharpened Nick's features. "Married?"

"Brooke introduced us. She didn't know about his wife and neither did I. He wasn't exactly forthcoming with that information."

Nick leaned his head back against the sofa. "Sounds like a great guy."

"I thought so at the time. He'd just moved to San Antonio from out of state to do a cardiology fellowship at Memorial. He was very attractive and charismatic and according to him, lonely. I made it my goal to make him feel welcome, and he made it his goal to charm my pants off, which he did."

That brought Nick's head back up. "When did you find out?"

"Months later. He left his cell phone at my house and I answered a call thinking it was him. It turned out to be the missus. Needless to say, we were both more than a little shocked to find out about the other. He left the hospital shortly after that. Packed up and moved back to his home in Maine and his wife, exactly how it should be. I haven't heard from him since, probably because I gave him a good piece of my mind." Not to mention a good piece of her heart.

"Must've been tough on you." Nick rubbed a hand down her arm in soft, soothing strokes, his tone understanding, not disparaging.

"Not really," she lied. "I just pulled myself up by my bootstraps and went on about my business." And pretended it hadn't hurt at all, when in reality it had devastated her.

"And it didn't bother you even a little bit?"

Michelle's guilt forced her gaze away from Nick. "Only from the standpoint that he said he cared about me, and it was nice to hear even if he didn't mean it. So I just chalk it up to my stupidity."

"You're not stupid, Michelle," he said adamantly, then more gently, "too trusting, maybe."

"*Was* too trusting," she corrected. "And he was a master at making a woman feel special, with lavish gifts and attention. Pretty words and smiles and—"

"Great sex?"

"Mediocre sex." Michelle's responding laugh was abrupt, humorless. "Granted, he was my first, so I didn't have anything to compare him to. But I honestly believe that he thought The Big *O* meant those giant mugs full of beer you get at half price during happy hour at the local sports bar."

"You're kidding, right?"

Michelle tipped her head back against the sofa and studied the exposed beams crisscrossing the ceiling. "Oh, that I were."

Nick's gentle fingers guided her face toward him. "The man's obviously an idiot in the first degree."

"He was smart in many ways. Just not in the right ways."

"And there's been no one since?"

Not until now. Not until Nick. "Nothing worth mentioning. I finally decided that I'm not that good at bringing out the best in a man."

Nick shifted until he came into closer contact with

her. He touched his lips to her forehead, then pulled back to study her face. "You're already bringing out the best in me."

The sincerity in his tone, his dark soulful eyes, made Michelle want to believe Nick. But past disappointments continued to shred her confidence. She acknowledged that she wanted to be with Nick yet protect herself against more disillusionment. Take pleasure in Nick's company and expect no more. It sounded simple enough.

But would it be so simple with a man like Nick Kempner? Yes, Nick was much the same as Brett in some basic ways—gorgeous, charming and persuasive. Brett had used those attributes to wear Michelle down, a little at a time. Nick hadn't put any pressure on her at all. On the contrary, he'd been insistent that they take it slow. Nick seemed honest and genuinely caring. But was it an act? She sincerely didn't think so, or maybe she didn't want to believe it.

For that reason Michelle had to remain focused on her current goal—enjoying Nick's company during the time they had together. No risk involved as long as she kept her heart out of the mix this time. But could she really do that? She had to for both their sakes.

Attempting to lighten the mood, she asked, "What is your idea of foreplay, Doctor?"

"You really want to know?"

You bet she did. "Yeah, so why don't you tell me?"

He bent closer to her ear and said in a deep, silken voice, "I'd rather show you."

He took a strawberry from her palm and bit it in half, then grazed it down her throat on to the valley between her breasts then back up again. Michelle shuddered at the contact, the tingles left in the berry's wake, the sudden rise in temperature that had nothing to do with the summer heat.

"You might believe that I don't live by many rules," he began, his voice deep and husky. "But I do, especially when it comes to making love."

He lowered his head and ran his softly abrading tongue along the path he'd made with the berry then studied her with dark, penetrating eyes. "On average, it takes fifteen minutes for a woman to reach a climax, and I consider that time well spent."

Michelle decided it would take her all of about two seconds if he kept this up. "Really? I didn't know that." Her voice was shrill and shaky, her body making demands that needed attention right here, right now.

"I'm not surprised, considering your former boy-friend." He wrapped his arm around her and held the half-eaten strawberry to her lips that she gladly took into her mouth. "Now, it's not an exact science, mind you. It depends on how it's accomplished."

She swallowed the bite with effort. "Meaning?"

"Whether I use my hands or my mouth."

Her body dissolved into liquid heat as if he'd used both on her. "Oh, my."

He smiled only halfway, then lowered his lips to her ear. "And that's what we have to look forward to, when you're ready."

She was more than ready. Ready to strip off her clothes and shove him down. Ready to force him to make good on his promise. "How long are you going to make me wait?"

"As long as it takes to convince you that I'm not looking for only a good time between the sheets."

That's all she was looking for at this point in her

life. At least she thought so. "I see. And how do you know that I'm not already convinced?"

His expression went from seductive to serious. "Because of your doubts about my character. Because of the things you've just told me. I want you to know up-front that I'm not *him.*"

"I wasn't making comparisons between you and Brett, if that's what you're thinking."

"Don't kid yourself, Michelle. That's exactly what you've been doing. And you're probably still doing it."

Darn his insight—and his stubbornness. Michelle was tired of talking. Tired of remembering. She wanted to forget. She wanted Nick to help her forget.

Michelle cupped Nick's raspy jaw in her palm. "You know, you're frustrating the heck out of me."

"You think I'm not frustrated?" He lowered his voice to a rough whisper. "I ache for you, Michelle. Right now it would take less than a minute to have you out of that robe so I could get inside you."

Her whole body reeled over that prospect. "I thought you needed fifteen minutes."

He chuckled. "You don't miss a thing, do you?"

She missed the feel of his lips. She craved them like some kissing addict. And his resistance be damned, she was going to get her Nick fix.

She pulled his head to hers and took his mouth with urgency, only beginning to alleviate her frustration. She half feared he would pull away, but he didn't. He held her closer and participated in the kiss with the same immediacy, thrusting his tongue in sinuous strokes between her parted lips until he had her longing for him to do the same with her needy body.

Without breaking the kiss, he let his hand drift down her throat to slip inside her robe. The moment suspended as she waited for his fingertips at her breast. When the moment didn't come, she wriggled her encouragement. He groaned against her lips before answering her plea to continue. His fingertips grazed her breast through the satin nightshirt, then he slipped his hand completely inside. He gently caressed and cajoled, fondled and finessed her bare flesh with soft touches, encouraging another rush of heat in Michelle's body.

But it only lasted a moment before he was sweeping her into his arms and heading up the stairs.

"Nick, where are we going?" As if she didn't know.

"I'm putting you to bed."

Funny, he hadn't said he was *taking* her to bed, exactly what she wanted him to do. Exactly what she needed him to do.

Instead, once they reached the bed, he laid her back on the comforter then stared down on her. "Go to sleep," he commanded.

She braced on her elbows, shocked by his sudden change of heart. "What did you say?"

"You need to sleep. I need a shower."

She lowered her gaze to the obvious swell beneath his fly. "That's not all you need."

He ran a hand over his jaw. "I'm okay."

She silently cursed his resistance. Cursed the realization that he was probably wise to put on the brakes. That didn't mean she had to like it. After all, tomorrow was another day, and another opportunity to wear Nick Kempner down. And wise or not, she wanted him. All of him. She'd face the consequences later. Much later.

"Okay, Nick, go take your shower," she said in her sweetest voice. "I'll go to sleep like a good girl. It should take me fifteen minutes, tops."

He rubbed a hand over his neck and studied the floor. "You are a bad girl, Michelle Lewis."

When he finally looked at her again, she gave him her best innocent smile. "I do know how to be good, though."

"Don't I know it." He turned toward the bathroom.

"Oh, Nick, one more thing."

He faced her again with a scowl and let go an impatient sigh. "Now what?"

"I hope I didn't use all the hot water during my shower."

He snapped off the overhead light, but before entering the bathroom, he said, "That's okay. I won't be needing any."

Nick took his time in the shower, worried that when he got out, Michelle would be in the next room lying in wait. Worried that this time he might not be able to refuse her because all the frigid water in the world couldn't stop the desire raging through him.

Worse, that desire went beyond the level of only the physical. The woman was truly a study in contradiction. He was only now beginning to realize that the person behind the confident persona had more than her share of heartache, thanks to some ruthless cheating bastard who gave all men a bad name. And with Nick's reputation at the hospital, no wonder Michelle didn't trust him.

Obviously, she was well versed at hiding her pain, her true feelings from the world. Unfortunately for him, she had chosen their time together to come out of her shell, engage in a little self-discovery, not only in a sexual sense but also in a determination to enjoy her freedom. A freedom that apparently had been lacking in her life due to her lousy past experience with love, the constraints of Brooke's illness, her parents' and her job's continued demands on her time.

Nick wanted to allow her that freedom. He wanted to aid her in that self-discovery and show her exactly what it meant to have a considerate lover. One that had all the time in the world to please her. But at what cost?

He'd planned to take things slowly, but their attraction—that indescribable spark—had begun to rush things forward at warp speed. He was helpless to stop it. If he tried, he might send the message to Michelle that she had no right to her freedom. Yet if he did let the relationship progress too quickly, he might find that when the passion faded, there would be nothing left to fall back on. He didn't want that. Nor did he want her to think for a minute that he was anything like that other jerk of a boyfriend, only out for a good time and nothing more—which couldn't be further from the truth.

For the first time in a long time, Nick was beginning to consider a serious relationship with a woman. A beautiful woman who liked his child and set his blood on fire with her untapped sensuality. A woman who had been selfless most of her life and deserved to have someone consider her needs for a change. Better still, a woman he enjoyed talking to and being with outside of bed. That was definitely a plus, and something totally new and different for him.

Tipping his head against the shower wall, he let the cold water wash over him in hopes of clearing his head and calming his body. It did neither. He might as well give up.

He shut off the faucet, dried his hair and body with

one towel then slipped another around his hips. He secured it at his waist, all he had to cover himself with
since his clean clothes were downstairs. Not much material between him and temptation.

Drawing in a deep breath, he opened the door to face
Michelle.

The bathroom light spilled over the bed where she
lay curled up facing him, fast asleep. He let out his
breath, but found he was almost disappointed, because
no matter how determined he was to proceed with caution, deep down he had hoped she would be waiting
for him, arms outstretched, asking him to come to her.

He leaned against the door frame and took a few
minutes to watch her. Her hands were tucked underneath her cheek, her slender shoulders bare and the
curve of her breasts in plain sight because of the
skimpy nightshirt. Her deep, steady breathing echoed
in the room, signaling she had probably been asleep
for a while now.

That realization brought Nick to the edge of the bed
where he quietly sat to gain a better view. She looked
as innocent as Kelsey, and so damned beautiful. He
wanted to touch her face, trace the outline of her dark
brows, which suddenly drew down toward her closed
lids in a frown. Her lips twitched for a moment, and
he thought she might actually say something. Probably
a few oaths directed at him, maybe all of mankind.

Something was disturbing her dreams, more than
likely memories of a doctor who'd torn up her heart.
If Nick were stronger, he'd climb into bed and hold
her. He didn't dare. If she rolled toward him during the
night, he wouldn't be able to resist her at all. And at
the moment he could at least buy a couple of days
before they complicated everything with lovemaking.

It could get really complicated if he allowed that to happen before she was ready. Before he convinced her that he was a man of honor.

Even so, he had absolutely no doubt in his mind where this was heading. Where they were heading.

Nick's fortitude was about to fail him as surely as he was about to fall—for Michelle Lewis. Maybe he already had.

Seven

The shaking mattress woke Michelle from the pleasant haze of a delightful dream of summer warmth on her face and crisp green grass beneath bare feet. And Nick.

She stretched and opened her eyes to find bright sunlight filtering into the room. She raised her head to see Nick bouncing the bed—with his hands.

Darn.

Obviously, it was morning. She'd tried so hard to stay awake last night—long enough to watch him leave the shower—but the minute her head had hit the pillow, she'd fallen asleep.

"Wake up, sleepyhead," he said. "It's almost noon."

She bolted upright. "Why did you let me sleep so long?"

"Because you needed it."

She needed to get up and get on with her day. She didn't need to squander any more time.

Michelle slipped from the bed and lifted her arms above her head for another stretch. Nick remained in the same spot near the end of the bed, but he moved his gaze over her in a long, slow caress. All her parts came awake then. Wide awake and raring to go.

"The boat's ready when you are," he said. "I've already packed our lunch and some drinks. All I need is you."

He seemed much too serious when he made the last declaration. Wouldn't it be nice to believe that she was all he needed? How silly to even consider that.

"Nick, you should've let me help you get ready."

"You're queen for the weekend, so enjoy it."

"Okay, but I'm starting to feel really worthless."

"I don't want to hear you say that again, you got it?"

Michelle was taken aback by the anger in his tone. She saluted. "Yes, Captain Kempner. I got it."

Michelle scooped up her robe from the floor, where it had obviously fallen from the end of the bed, probably after some heavy-duty tossing and turning. Funny, she didn't remember moving an inch during the night. "I'll just freshen up and change into my suit, then I'll meet you downstairs," she said.

He didn't move for a moment. He simply continued to stare at her, as if he wanted to say something else.

Finally he said, "Okay," then sprinted down the stairs.

Michelle made quick work in the bathroom and changed into her black bikini. She stepped back and took a look in the floor-length mirror positioned on the back of the door.

She certainly looked washed out. What little tan she'd managed to get this summer had already faded. The bruise at her side was now yellow, and ugly. Maybe she should opt to wear a tent. Unfortunately, she hadn't brought one.

Nope, she'd just have to settle for what she had brought, a sheer black cover-up. After slipping on the cover-up and her sandals, then stuffing her mesh beach bag with a towel and tanning oil, she headed down-stairs to find Nick.

She followed the smells of coffee into the kitchen and found him sitting at the table, reading the paper. He didn't bother to look up, so Michelle went to the coffeemaker, took a mug from the mug tree and poured it to near overflowing. She definitely needed some cof-fee to wake up completely. Not that Nick wasn't help-ing her out with that.

Facing the counter, she added sugar and lots of cream to her coffee. During the process, she sneaked a glance at Nick. His near-raven hair was sensually mussed, and he obviously hadn't shaved from the looks of his shaded jaw. The light-blue tank he wore did little to cover the spattering of crisp dark hair on his chest. And, oh, the man did things to swim trunks that really shouldn't be allowed, at least not for a woman who was engaged in a mighty tough struggle with her hor-mones, warring to keep her eyes above his waist.

She turned toward him, gripping the cup with her sweaty palm. "Want some?"

His gaze shot to hers. "Huh?"

She held up her cup. "Coffee?"

Nick conducted another visual search down her body, a bit quicker this time, before dropping the open newspaper into his lap. "Nope, I've had enough. Several cups while you were still in la-la land."

"You really should've woken me up," she scolded. "And I really should consider calling work to check up on things."

He stood and tossed the newspaper aside. "No way. Whatever comes up, you'll have to handle it on Monday."

Monday. What an ugly day of the week. She didn't even want to think about that now, not while she was with Nick. Not until she absolutely had to. "Okay, Mr. Boss Man. What now?"

Finally he smiled. "To the boat. I've got to warn you, though, it's pretty hot out there."

If Michelle really decided to go through with her plan, it would probably get even hotter.

Nick took Michelle's hand and helped her onto the dock where he had moored the boat earlier that morning. It was the first time he'd touched her, not that he hadn't wanted to. In fact, it had taken all his will not to crawl into bed and wake her in some very inventive ways. Or to take her back to bed when she'd showed up in the kitchen wearing that black sheer thing that covered her about as well as plastic wrap. But not after her revelations last night. Now, more than ever, he would set out to prove himself to her.

After a mental pep talk on the virtues of self-control, Nick untied the boat from the dock and pushed off. In his peripheral vision he could see Michelle standing next to the passenger seat, slipping the cover-up from her slender shoulders to unveil her bikini. He took his seat behind the wheel with a quick glance at Michelle before staring straight ahead to keep from staring at her.

"What's in there?" she asked, pointing at the closed bow in front of them.

A place that could mean trouble for both of them. "It's a cuddy cabin. There's some cushions and a portable head underneath those. It's kind of small, but it's equipped in case you want to spend the night on the water."

She grinned. "A floating bedroom. How nice."

To her it might seem that way, yet he'd never used it as anything but a convenience for his daughter on family outings. A place for Kelsey to nap while he and Bridget sat in silence, struggling to find something to say. Not once had he and Bridget utilized it for anything else, namely lovemaking.

He pushed the ignition and turned the key to start the boat. "It came in handy with Kelsey," he said, wishing all the old garbage would float away as easily as he guided the boat beyond the dock.

Michelle took her place on the passenger seat while they passed the No Wake zone and out onto the lake. Nick pushed the throttle and the boat roared to life as he headed for his favorite cove. Lake traffic was light but it would definitely get worse the following day. And on Saturday, the weekend vacationers would come out in droves like fire ants to create a near traffic jam on the water. But today he planned to take advantage of the solitude and his time with Michelle, alone on the lake.

He glanced at her now and then, the wind whipping her long silky hair behind her, her blue eyes hidden behind sunshades. She turned her face to the sun, presenting a great view of her profile—the slightly upturned nose, the small chin, the long column of her delicate throat. She smiled and held her arms out to her sides like a bird that had suddenly been emancipated from its cage.

Nick tried to avoid going any further with his observations, but he didn't have the will. His gaze took in the swell of her breasts, barely covered by the black satin bikini, her flat abdomen, shapely thighs and legs.

Her body was made for worshipping, and if he didn't keep his eyes straight ahead, they were in danger of running ashore.

A few minutes later Nick turned left into the secluded cove surrounded by a decent beach and quite a few trees, a water skier's paradise on weekends, but luckily not today.

After dropping anchor a few hundred yards from shore, he turned to Michelle, who was trying to maneuver the seat back where it would form one long bench. A place to lie down. A dangerous place.

"How do you work this thing?" she asked with a frown.

"Hang on, I'll get it." With one easy move he pushed the seat back. "How's that?"

"Great." She faced him, bent over and rummaged around in her bag, giving Nick a bird's-eye view of the tops of her breasts. He couldn't seem to tear his gaze away.

"I've got it," she declared.

So did he. Bad. For her. "What?"

"Tanning oil." Sitting on the edge of the bench, she opened the bottle and began applying it to her skin— over her shoulders, the tops of her breasts, then down her belly with slow torturous strokes.

Now Nick was in danger of embarrassing himself.

Turning away, he headed toward the back of the boat, stripping off his shirt as he went. Without any explanation, he dove overboard from the swim deck.

The water was relatively cool, but not cold enough. He surfaced to find Michelle with arms folded atop the edge, leaning over, emphasizing her cleavage to its best advantage. "You should have told me you wanted to swim. I would've joined you."

That's the last thing he needed. "Just wanted to cool off." Unfortunately, he hadn't.

"Okay. Come back and see me when you're done. I need your help."

He didn't dare ask with what. "In a minute."

He swam a few strokes toward the middle of the lake, determined to expend some energy. Maybe he could make himself too tired to touch her. Not likely.

After a time he hoisted himself back in the boat to find Michelle lying on her belly—Michelle stretched out like a coddled cat, all legs and lines and luscious curves. "Mind putting some oil on my back?" she asked him over one shoulder.

Did he mind? Not hardly, but he really shouldn't. "Just a minute. I'm going to get a drink. Want something?"

"Do you have any water?"

He headed for the built-in cooler on the other side. "Yeah. I brought plenty. It's nice and cold." Maybe he should just dump a bottle down his trunks.

He handed her the water, took a long drink of his sports drink, then went to his knees beside her. He put down the plastic bottle and picked up the tanning oil from the floor, preparing to rub Michelle. Her back, he corrected. Man, he hoped he survived.

Then she reached behind her with both hands, headed for the strap and gave it a solid twist.

Don't do it, Michelle…

Too late.

She snapped the back strap open, then untied the string at her neck. For all intents and purposes, she was bare from the hips up. And Nick was just this side of jumping overboard again.

Things only got worse when he began to apply the oil. Her skin, warmed by the sun, was satin smooth beneath his fingertips as he rubbed the liquid slowly across her shoulders, down her spine. A good straight spine. At least he had the presence of mind to slip back into doctor mode for a minute. But that didn't last when his hands traveled around to her sides.

"I think my bruise looks better," she said, her words muffled since her face was resting on her crossed arms.

"Yeah? I haven't even noticed it." Plenty more to notice without looking for a bruise.

She glanced back at him with a wily grin. "Want to check it out better?" Before he could answer, she braced herself upright on bent elbows. Nick saw a flash of the bottom curve of her breast and cursed.

"You turn over, and I guarantee I won't be looking at your bruise," he growled.

"Really? What will you be looking at?"

"Stop playing with me, Michelle."

Her grin expanded. "Is that what I'm doing?"

"You know exactly what you're doing." She was still doing it and quite sufficiently.

The low rumble of a motor caught Nick's attention. He looked to his right to see a bass boat trolling near the bank.

Michelle started to raise herself up but he pushed her

shoulder back. "Don't move," he said in a harsh command.

She looked back at him with a frown. "Why? Haven't you seen a bare-breasted woman before?"

Plenty, but he didn't want anyone else looking at Michelle. "There's a couple of fisherman to our right. They both look to be in their seventies, and I'm not sure their tickers could take it if you flash them, and I'm sure as heck not in the mood to play doctor at the moment."

"Sorry. I didn't hear anything." She reached in her nearby bag and withdrew a towel, shimmied it underneath her chest, then sat up. Nick got off his knees and sat beside her.

She regarded him a long moment before saying, "Maybe we should go into the cabin. Just until they leave." She patted his bare thigh. "We can see what comes up."

"Michelle, you have more determination in your little finger than most people have in their whole bodies."

"Maybe, but it's not my little finger that needs attention."

Nick laughed a mirthless laugh. He was in too much pain to be overly jolly. He tried one last time to bring out all his arguments. Give her one last shot at changing her mind before it was too late. "There's not much room in there."

"Do we need that much room?"

She had a point. So did he. "It's pretty warm, even when you open the hatch."

"And it's not out here?"

"Baby, right now I could set these seats on fire."

She shot a glance at the fishermen, then pulled the towel away for a brief moment, flashing Nick.

That did it. He hooked his arms under her legs, picked her up, struggled with the doors, then scooted her into the cabin and onto the cushions. He yanked away the towel so he could feel her bare breasts pressed against his chest when he kissed her. And boy, did he kiss her.

All of Nick's pent-up sexual energy came out in that kiss as he took her mouth with no mercy. Not that she wasn't holding her own. He stopped only to open the hatch above, giving them more oxygen. He really needed it at the moment.

He stared at her translucent blue eyes, her oil-slick body, the rise and fall of her teardrop breasts and fought not to strip off all their clothes and get down to business.

Surprisingly she blushed under his continued perusal. "You think I'm crazy, don't you?"

He followed the curve of her hip with one greedy hand. "No. Not at all."

She looked away. "I don't know how to explain this. I'm never, ever like this. All of the sudden I feel like a rubber band ready to snap. It even sounds crazy."

Nick traced the line of her jaw, drawing her attention back to him. "Michelle, it's my professional opinion, as a physician, that you're suffering from that malady known as horniness."

She slapped his arm. "That sounds so crude."

He tried hard to look serious, mock professional. "Crude, but normal. After all, you told me that it's been three years. You have certain biological needs. It's nothing to be ashamed of. Nothing that can't be cured."

"Thanks so much for your expert opinion, Doctor. Now what do you suggest I do to cure this condition?"

He ran his knuckles over her belly, slowly back and forth, allowing his fingertips to travel only a fraction underneath the bikini band below her navel. "It might cost you."

She gasped when his hand moved farther beneath the material. "I'm willing to pay."

"Great. Just leave it all up to me then."

Nick bent and took one tawny nipple between his lips and sent his hand completely inside the bikini bottoms. Her chest rose hard beneath his mouth as he explored the reaches of her warm, soft flesh with his fingertips, searching for the place that would have her begging. If he didn't beg first.

Nick found the spot, eliciting a gasp from Michelle. He lifted his head from her breasts, rolled to his side and rested his jaw on his palm to watch her. She raised her arms above her head and closed her eyes. When he quickened his touch, she turned her face away from him. He would have none of that. He wanted her to know it was him touching her, and to never forget it.

Slipping his arm underneath Michelle's neck, Nick nudged her face back toward him. Her blue eyes fluttered open, hazy with need. The first word that came to Nick's mind was rapture. That pretty much summed up the look on her face.

Nick was thankful for the sunlight that allowed him to see this moment. He whispered in her ear, letting her know how good she felt. How beautiful she looked. How much he wanted her.

Her bottom lip quivered, her eyes drifted shut, and he slid one finger inside her the moment she shattered, feeling the tiny pulsations, wishing he were buried deep inside her.

Nick removed his hand from beneath the bikini and held Michelle until her breathing steadied. Held her for what seemed like an eternity, the boat gently rocking with only the sound of lapping water interrupting the quiet. He didn't mind allowing her this time to recover. After all, he was only beginning to make her feel good.

She remained surprisingly still. For some reason he expected her to tear off his trunks and beg him to finish. Or maybe that's what he was wishing she would do, because at the moment his body demanded relief.

Instead she remained quiet. He hoped she wasn't feeling guilty. But as he lifted his head once again to look at her, he suddenly realized that wasn't it at all.

She was sound asleep.

Nick wasn't sure if he should be proud or insulted. He'd like to think that having this release had relaxed her so much that she had simply drifted off. After all, she was exhausted. After all, that's why they had come here to the lake, so she could get some much-needed R and R.

Well, at least one of them was.

Bolting upright, Michelle bumped her head on the top of the low ceiling. She took a minute to focus, to reorient herself to place and time. She heard the steady hum of a motor, felt the gentle rocking like a baby's cradle, took one look at her half-naked body and suddenly realized exactly where she was and exactly what had happened.

She'd fallen asleep. Fallen asleep after Nick Kempner had taken her straight to paradise with his skilled touch.

Mortification seeped in when she considered having to face Nick. She couldn't imagine what he thought of her now, but she assumed *selfish* would be one word he'd use to describe her behavior. Unfortunately, she would have to find out, unless she decided to spend the rest of the weekend hiding out in the closet-size cabin.

The motor shut off and the boat bumped, jarring her into action. Slowly she pushed open the cabin doors to sneak a peek and saw Nick tying the boat to the dock. Michelle's face blazed and it had nothing to do with the atmosphere. In fact, it appeared to be nearing dusk, the setting sun much lower in the sky than it had been when they'd entered the boat's cabin. How long had she been asleep? And why in heaven's name had he let her continue the nap indefinitely? Better still, how could she have done something so stupid, with Nick Kempner in her arms willing to give her exactly what she'd been waiting for?

Michelle snatched up the nearby towel, secured it around her bare torso and climbed out of the cabin. Head lowered, she found her cover-up and bikini top then returned to the cabin to put them on. When she came out dressed but still embarrassed, Nick stood on the dock holding two sacks, presumably containing their lunch—the lunch they hadn't eaten, thanks to her botched seduction and untimely nap.

She wanted to run the other direction instead of facing Nick. A very cowardly thing to do, not to mention the lake was behind her and she wasn't practiced at running on water. Instead she lifted her chin, grabbed up her bag and joined him on the dock.

"Did you have a nice nap?" he asked, but his smile was absent.

"I'm sorry, Nick. It's just that…" *I'm an idiot.*

"It's okay, Michelle. You're tired. Since you didn't have any lunch, I'll make dinner as soon as we get back to the house."

"Did you have lunch?" she asked with concern.

He turned and started up the path leading to the cabin. "Yeah, I had a bite. I swam some, too."

"You should have woken me up."

"You needed your rest."

She needed him to understand how brainless she felt. How much she still wanted him. She hurried to catch up with him. "I really am sorry." When he didn't stop or bother to look at her she said, "Nick, can we talk about this?"

He glanced at her but kept walking at a fast clip. "We'll talk later. Right now you need something to eat."

Darn his insistence on treating her like a child who needed a keeper. Of course, she had acted like a child, falling asleep like some two-year-old after one of the most incredible experiences of her life.

Nothing she could do about that now. But she could make it up to Nick somehow, and she would, *if* he ever slowed down.

When they reached the house, Nick sent Michelle to the shower and himself to the kitchen to start dinner. He needed some distance, time to regroup. He hoped like hell she came back dressed in something less revealing, as if that could stifle his urge to carry her to bed and finish what they'd started on the boat.

Later, he thought. Right now he needed time to think. Time to plan. If he chose to view Michelle's spontaneous nap logically, he should be happy that he'd at least made her feel good without disrupting his plan to take their relationship slowly. But logic wasn't foremost on his mind. Desire was.

He needed to slam on the brakes, start over. Make sure that she was really ready to go all the way, and that meant beyond the weekend, not necessarily just sex. He wanted Michelle; he couldn't deny that. But he wanted more. Exactly what *more* meant, he didn't have a clue at the moment. Maybe just more time with her after they returned to the city. Maybe more than a few dates. Maybe *more* as in *long-term.*

That thought stopped him cold in the middle of tossing a salad. Man, he was jumping the gun. He had to stop and assess his next move or risk running her off for good.

After firing up the grill on the back deck, he slapped two T-bones on to cook, then went back into the house to make some margaritas. His first impulse was to indulge in a few straight shots of the tequila in hopes of discouraging his libido. Not a good idea. He hadn't done shots since college, and that conjured up some bad memories he didn't care to relive. He sure as heck didn't think that would impress Michelle. Besides, she was much more intoxicating than liquor.

He popped two potatoes into the microwave and carried the pitcher of margaritas to the redwood table. Before he could sit, Michelle came out the patio doors smelling sweet and looking even sweeter. She wore a sleeveless yellow sundress and a self-conscious smile.

"Can I help?" she asked.

Quite a few ways that she could help entered Nick's mind, but none had to do with dinner. "Everything's all set." He pointed to the pitcher. "Do you want a drink?"

She gracefully slid onto the bench across from him. "Sure."

He poured the mix into a salt-rimmed mug and sat it before her, then poured himself one and took his seat.

She held the glass up to the dim porch light. "Is this your famous margarita?"

"Yeah, my very own recipe."

She took a slow drink, then licked the salt from the bottom of her full lip. "Very good. Maybe you should market this. You know, in case you decide to retire from medicine."

He cleared his throat and controlled his urge to kiss the salt away slowly from her mouth. "Not likely that's going to happen anytime soon. At least I hope not."

Leaning forward with her hands circled around the mug, she smiled. "I take it you love what you're doing."

He loved the way she looked at him, her flame-blue eyes reflecting the overhead light, the crease of her dimple. He loved...her?

Pushing aside that disconcerting thought, he said, "Medicine's everything to me."

"Everything?"

"Well, now that you mention it, not everything. Kelsey's everything. She's the reason I get up every day and go to work, even when it's the last thing I want to do."

Michelle's soft sigh floated on the warm breeze. "She's lucky to have you as her dad."

"She has a great mom, too."

"How nice to hear you say that in light of your problems with your ex-wife... What's her name?"

He didn't want to talk about his failed marriage, but

he figured he'd left himself wide open by mentioning his ex to Michelle. "Her name is Bridget."

"Oh. Nice name." She said it with little enthusiasm, and maybe even with a hint of jealousy.

"She's a good woman, Michelle. Just because we couldn't make it work doesn't make her a bad person."

She frowned. "I didn't say she was a bad person. I'd never pass judgment on someone I don't even know."

Nothing like screwing up right out of the gate this evening. "I know that. Sometimes I worry people think that I despise her because of our messy divorce. It was pretty much public knowledge that we didn't get along in the end, but we're trying to be friends now."

"Do you really put that much stock in what other people think?"

"I try not to, but it's hard at times. For Kelsey's sake I want everyone to think we had an amicable parting."

"Very noble of you, Dr. Kempner." Michelle held up her glass for a toast. "Here's to amicable partings."

Nick wasn't sure he wanted to toast to that. Was she referring to him and Bridget, or was she already planning a friendly exit after their time together ended?

No way would he let that happen, at least not without a fight.

Raising his glass, he sent her a determined look. "Here's to new beginnings."

Eight

Michelle struggled all through dinner to come to terms with Nick's cryptic toast. What did he want from her? Did he intend for them to have a long-term relationship? A call-every-day-and-see-each-other-every-night kind of thing? Or had she misinterpreted his intent? And if that was what he intended, could she trust him, trust herself to pursue a relationship at the risk of having it end badly?

Michelle sat alone on the sofa and waited for Nick to return from his shower. Waited with confusing thoughts crowding her brain. Even after a half hour of pondering the recent events, she had come up with few answers.

Let's face it, she thought. Nick didn't really know her at all. He didn't know the chronic relationship bumbler she could be. He didn't know all her secrets, the insecurities she harbored like last season's clothes with which she couldn't seem to part. He didn't know that she was a sad case when it came to matters of the heart.

Regardless, she did want him on a very basic level. She wanted all that he would give her from a physical standpoint. She couldn't afford to want more. Little by little, she had let loose her inhibitions, but that was as far as she could go with Nick Kempner, a man who had more charm than should be allowed. A man who was sought after by many women. A doctor with revered status in the medical field and a reputation for being the love-'em-and-leave-'em kind. She'd been left before and, although Nick appeared to be honorable, she didn't have the courage to trust her instincts again. They had already failed her once. Love was simply out of the question.

Footfalls on the stairs forced Michelle to look back. Nick strode toward her wearing a short-sleeved shirt completely unbuttoned and a pair of tattered cutoff jeans. His hair was shower damp, and his smile illuminated the dimly lit room.

"Feeling better?" she asked in the most casual tone she could muster in light of the fact that her pulse thrummed in a staccato rhythm.

"I feel cleaner." He slid onto the sofa and propped his heels on the table in front of them. He didn't bother to button his shirt, providing a nice distraction for Michelle. Very nice indeed.

He smelled great, like soap and something else. Shaving cream, Michelle decided when she noted his smooth jaw. She couldn't make up her mind which way she liked him better—clean shaven or sensually shaded with whiskers. Either way suited her just fine.

Michelle moved a little closer but kept a slight distance. After her behavior in the boat, she didn't want him to think she was ready to pounce if given the opportunity. Not yet, anyway.

Bending her knees, she rested her heels on the edge of the sofa, pulled her hem down to midcalf and hugged her legs to her chest. "Should we watch a movie?" She nodded toward the shelf in the corner. "I noticed you have quite a collection of videos."

"Yeah, if you like purple dinosaurs and fairies. Most of those are Kelsey's favorites."

She glanced his way. "No adult entertainment?"

"Not here."

She tried to look shocked. "Dr. Kempner, are you saying you have naughty movies at your apartment?"

He frowned. "Not any eight-millimeter movies that arrive in a brown paper bag, if that's what you're insinuating. In fact, nothing more than an R rating. Most of those are action flicks. Blood and guts. Sizable body counts."

Michelle wrinkled her nose. "No, thanks. I prefer light romantic comedies."

"Sorry to disappoint you."

He was anything but disappointing her, even considering his questionable taste in movies and his sudden unreadable mood. "I'm not disappointed." At least not yet.

A long span of silence passed before Nick spoke again. "Michelle, there's something I need to say to you."

Oh, boy. Was she really ready to hear it, whatever "it" might be? If his serious tone was any indication, she might not care much for what he was about to say. "Go ahead."

He dropped his feet from the table and leaned forward with hands clasped on his thighs. "After we leave here, I don't want this to be over between us."

Not exactly what she had expected, but exactly what she'd feared. "I think that's a bit premature, don't you? We still have until Sunday to make that decision."

"I've already made my decision." He pinned her with a dark, soulful gaze. "I think we could have a really good thing going, if you'll let down your guard and talk to me."

Michelle hugged her knees closer to her chest. "I thought that's what we've been doing."

"I mean *really* talking. We've danced around the issues, and I think we need to get to the point. I know you're worried about why I divorced Bridget, and I don't blame you."

Considering her history, yes she was worried. More than she should be. "Look, Nick, I'm not naive. People get divorced for all kinds of reasons. I'm sure yours were valid."

"Then you'll consider seeing me after this weekend?"

She didn't know what to say, what to feel. Fear clamped down hard on her heart. "I don't know, Nick. I'm not very good at relationships."

"Neither am I, but I want to give us a shot."

A much too serious topic, in Michelle's opinion. She didn't want to have to think about the future, only the present.

Taking a huge chance, Michelle draped her legs over the edge of the sofa and moved closer to him. "Can't we wait and see what happens? Just enjoy each other's company for the time being?"

Nick leaned his head back and sighed. "If you mean can we just make love and forget the rest, I can't."

"Why not?"

He turned his face to her, his expression dead serious. "Because I did that once. I had great sex with a woman and I married her. After the excitement faded, we had nothing left but our daughter."

The sadness in his voice stole Michelle's breath. "Sex does complicate things, doesn't it?"

"Yeah, it does."

"But does it really have to?"

"I guess it doesn't if you don't care about the person you're with. I don't want that kind of hollow relationship anymore. I've been there, done that, too many times."

So had Michelle, although it had only been once. Once was enough. "But how do you know if it's right? Do you ever really know a person completely?"

He cupped her jaw and turned her face toward him. "I think it takes more than a weekend to get to know someone. But I'm not sure it takes all that long to know when something's right."

Her heart executed a little hip-hop in her chest. She pushed back the hasty hope that tried to intercept her common sense. "Right as in sex, or right as in a serious relationship?"

He brushed a kiss over her lips. "Maybe both."

She felt a soul-slicing fear. "I think it's way too early to consider happily-ever-after."

"You might be right about that, but I think it's worth exploring." He leaned back against the sofa after sending her an impatient look. "You don't have to decide anything now. I just thought I'd mention it so you know where I stand."

"I appreciate that."

Michelle snuggled closer to his side but tried her best

to maintain some emotional distance. She circled a fin-gertip round and round over his bare chest. "Does this mean we have to forgo lovemaking until I decide?"

Nick groaned. "Michelle, you're making this hard on me."

She grinned. "Oh, goody. I hope so."

Determined to take the doctor's mind off the talk of expectations, Michelle tugged the snap open on his fly.

"What are you doing?" he asked, his voice little more than a croak.

"Research." She tracked his zipper down slowly.

"Research?"

"I want to see if the fifteen-minute rule applies to men."

"Take my word for it, it doesn't."

"No offense, but I have to prove it for myself." She shimmied his shorts and briefs down his narrow hips, revealing all to her eyes. But she didn't have time to enjoy the sight for fear he would stop her. Or maybe she might lose her nerve. She'd never even attempted this before. She only hoped that she could do it justice, if Nick allowed it.

She planted a kiss in the middle of his chest then worked her lips slowly downward.

When she reached the taut plane of his abdomen right below his navel, his breath hissed out like steam from a radiator.

He twined his fingers through her hair and molded her scalp. "You're killing me, Michelle."

She certainly didn't intend to kill him, only subject him to a little persuasive torture. But the effect Nick's reaction was having on her equaled the one she was having on him. A steady pressure began to build in intimate places as she slowly headed toward her destination with featherlight kisses. She'd barely reached her goal when Nick pulled her head up, stood, tugged on his shorts and briefs then scooped her into his arms. He headed for the stairs before she had time to issue a protest.

"Where are we going?"

He took the stairs two at a time. "To bed."

Not again. Not if she could help it. "I swear, Nick Kempner, you better not mean you're putting me to bed for the night. I'm not the least bit tired."

"No, I'm taking you to bed. You've started something, and I intend to finish it."

She wanted to let loose a victory cheer. *Go, Nick! Go!* A silly idea, but at the moment she felt a little giddy. "I'm thinking you don't intend for us to go to sleep, then."

"Lady, you've got that right."

Nine

For Nick the day of reckoning had arrived. D-Day. Payday. Ground zero.

If he had any intentions of stopping, he'd better do it now before it was too late. Before he laid Michelle down and proceeded to take the ultimate gamble by making mindless love to her all night. Before he took that leap of faith, risking that he could very well fall...head over heels in love.

She didn't afford him the opportunity to put a halt to what they were about to do. After he set her on her feet, she tugged him to the bed. They tumbled down together in a tangle of limbs to the sound of Michelle's carefree laughter. Nick didn't feel like laughing, not when his body raged with need. Not with the prospect of being inside Michelle and taking them both to the limit. Not when he was about to take this final step, possibly making one colossal mistake and putting their relationship in peril.

But stopping was no longer an option. He couldn't think with Michelle beneath him, twisting her hips against his groin until he thought he might explode. She continued to take the lead when she rose up and worked the dress over her head, leaving her clad in only white silk bra and panties.

When Michelle nudged him onto his back, Nick didn't have the will to resist. In fact, he more than appreciated the freedom after she relieved him of his gaping shirt, shorts and briefs.

He managed to catch her wrist before she landed her hands on the intended target now exposed in all its glory. "If you even so much as touch me, Michelle, we're running the risk that this whole experience is going to be over in less time than it took to get you up the stairs."

Grinning, she rolled onto her side, rose up on one elbow and rested her cheek on her palm. "Okay, now that I know this won't take fifteen minutes, I've mentally calculated that we can achieve quite a bit of research before morning."

"Oh, yeah. I plan on achieving a lot of things." He pushed her onto her back and rose above her. "Just one more thing. I realize that doctors have this all-powerful persona, but I have to warn you, I'll need some time to recover."

She frowned. "Not much time, I hope."

"Greedy, aren't we?"

"You could say that. Just let me know when you're ready."

"You'll know when I'm ready."

Nick intended to let her know a lot of things, namely

that he wasn't done with her yet. Not by a long shot. He started by slipping her bra and panties away, slowly. She squirmed some more. He really liked making her squirm. Before he was done, he anticipated making her writhe. And maybe even making her scream.

But first things first. He withdrew a condom from the nightstand and placed it on top within immediate reach.

She turned her head toward the plastic package, and her eyes widened with childlike wonder. "Oh, can I do it?"

Nick laughed. "If you're a good girl, but not yet."

She stuck out her bottom lip in a pretend pout. "Are you going to make me wait another fifteen minutes, after all?"

"Believe me, you won't last that long."

"Promise?"

"If you say please."

"Pretty please?"

He ran his tongue along her pouting bottom lip. "With sugar on top."

Holding her wrists above her head, he kissed her earnestly, exploring the ridges of her perfect teeth with his tongue before sliding it into the warmth of her mouth. He put his all into the kiss, gliding between her parted lips with long slow strokes, then withdrawing even slower to increase the tension. He couldn't remember ever being so tense, balanced on the brink of totally losing control.

He worked his way from her neck to her breasts with more wet kisses, then sucked a nipple into his mouth and drew lazy circles with his tongue. She moaned her pleasure. He wanted to join her in some moaning of his own. Instead he continued on his trek downward, drawing a line with his tongue to her navel. He skimmed his hands down her raised arms to cup her breasts before continuing on to the curve of her waist, the arc of her hip and finally to her long legs, which he bent at the knees and parted to accommodate him.

Michelle gasped when he found the ultimate goal with his mouth.

She was so sweet. So soft and warm and wet. So willing. Everything he could ask for in a lover, and almost more than he could take as a man.

With no more effort than a few intimate kisses, she shook with the force of her climax. She also screamed.

Nick felt pleased and proud—and ready to ignite. He kissed his way back up Michelle's body, and when he raised his head he found her clutching the condom in her hand.

"Are we ready now?" She sounded winded and determined.

"Babe, I don't think *ready* comes close to describing my current state."

"Good." Tearing open the condom, she nudged him onto his back and had it in place in record time.

He moved over her then and slipped inside her, seating himself deep in her heat. The sudden overwhelming sensations caused Nick to pause and evaluate. What was so different about making love to Michelle? Why was *she* so different from the rest? Why did he have this inexplicable weight in his chest and the need to tell her how much this meant to him?

He wasn't given to emotional revelations. Hell, he wasn't good with words at all. Bridget had told him that on more than one occasion. No need to ruin the moment by voicing feelings that he couldn't begin to understand.

When he failed to move, Michelle said, "Nick, is something wrong?"

No, everything was right. Almost too right. "It's okay, Michelle. I need some time in order to do this justice."

"Okay, as long as you really want this." Her voice sounded weak, uncertain.

He gave her a reassuring kiss on her cheek. "Believe me, I *really* want it."

If she only knew how much it was costing him to take his time, she wouldn't doubt for a minute that he wanted her. Wanted her with everything in him. He withdrew a bit then sank back into her. His body demanded a wild and reckless rhythm, his brain cautioned him to take it slow. Unfortunately, his body won out despite the fact he tried to temper his movements. But when Michelle wrapped her long legs around his waist and met him thrust for thrust, nature took over without regard for patience.

Sending his hands down Michelle's body, Nick memorized the feel of her, every curve, every crevice. He kissed her again, making love to her mouth with fluid strokes of his tongue. She released a needy sound against his lips. He could relate. He couldn't remember ever needing something—or *someone*—so much.

With a few deliberate touches, a few practiced moves, he brought her to another release. He savored the feel of her surrounding him, drawing him farther into her welcoming body. He appreciated the knowledge that he had provided her with more pleasure. He gladly accepted the pain of her nails digging into his back, something that might provide an anchor in this storm of emotions building deep inside. But it was no use. He was as lost as he had ever been.

He didn't have time to analyze the concept. The climax ripped through him, launching every coherent thought from his brain. He gave in to the moment and immersed himself in sheer sensation.

The moments to follow were some of the best, and worst, at least for Nick. Worst because it was over. Best because it didn't have to be the last time tonight. Best because he didn't remember ever feeling so good. Worst because everything had changed between them, and maybe not necessarily for the better. *He* had definitely changed, in some very unexpected ways.

Making love with Michelle had brought about the realization that something had been missing from his life. That "something" happened to be Michelle, and if he had his way, he wouldn't be without her ever again.

If this was real love, then he'd fallen into it big-time.

Ten

Without thinking, Michelle snatched up the ringing phone that had so irritatingly disturbed her sleep.

"H'lo?"

"Shelly?"

"Mom?" Michelle bolted from the bed and pushed her hair from her face.

"No, silly. It's Brooke. Please don't tell me that I'm starting to sound like Mom. I've already inherited her hips."

Michelle perched on the edge of the bed and pushed her tousled hair out of her face. "Sorry. I'm not quite with it yet this morning."

"My gosh, Shelly. It's almost noon. Were you still sleeping?"

"As a matter of fact, I was."

"That surprises me. You've always been such an early riser."

Nick had been an early riser, the reason why Michelle had been sound asleep. They had made love again not more than an hour ago, and she was suffering the effects with some pleasantly sore spots all over her body.

"I'm taking it easy, Brooke, just like you told me I should." Taking it however she could get it with Nick, and she had gotten it. Three times.

"Glad to hear it, Michelle."

"Tell your sister to get to the point, I need your assistance," Nick grumbled.

A long silence filled the line while Michelle futilely tried to bat Nick's hand away from her bare breast. She hadn't even noticed that he'd moved.

"Is that who I think it is, Shelly?" Brooke asked in a singsong voice.

Michelle looked back at Nick stretched out on his back, naked and beautifully masculine. Beautiful, period. "It's the milkman, Brooke. Who do you think?"

Brooke chuckled. "Oh, my gosh, you got some, didn't you?"

"Some milk?"

"Sex, you numbskull," Brooke said in a voice that could shake the walls. "Was it great? Details, Michelle. I need details."

Nick rolled to his side and snatched the phone from Michelle's hand. "I'm the best she's ever had, we plan to stay in bed the rest of the day, and is there anything else you want to know, Brooke, so we can get back to it?"

Frowning, Michelle tugged the phone away and turned her back on Nick's sexy grin and gorgeous body before she tossed the phone aside to attack him once again. "Sorry about that. Why are you calling me, any-way?"

"Just checking...up on you." Even through the phone line, Michelle could hear Brooke struggling for breath.

"Brooke, are you okay?"

"Yeah, I'm okay. How are you?" Brooke let go a round of harsh, wheezing coughs. She sounded horrible to Michelle, unearthing all the recollections of the troublesome asthma attacks Brooke had suffered during their childhood, reviving Michelle's unabated fear for her sister's well-being.

Michelle sprang from the bed, slipped on her robe and started to pace along the loft's railing. "Brooke, it's your asthma, isn't it?"

"It's nothing, Michelle."

Sudden anger pelted Michelle like a torrential rain. "It's *nothing?* Your asthma is *nothing?* It's never been nothing. Ever."

"You worry too much, Shelly."

She sent a glance in Nick's direction. He'd put on a pair of pajama bottoms and had stretched out on his back again, one arm draped over his eyes as if he'd fallen back to sleep. Or perhaps he was only pretending not to listen. Regardless, Michelle started toward the stairs.

"You know something, Brooke. Maybe you don't worry enough. Might I remind you that you're pregnant?"

"You don't need to remind me. I'm living it every day. I have a huge belly and swollen feet, not to mention my big butt."

Ignoring Brooke's attempt to make light of her illness, Michelle walked down the stairs and took a seat on the bottom step, hopefully out of Nick's earshot. "Might I also remind you how sick you can get if you don't take care of yourself? It's not only you now, Brooke. Think about your baby. You still have over two months to go. You need to stay healthy."

"I am thinking about my baby, and I'm fine."

"Are you really, or are you lying to me and yourself?"

"What's wrong with you? Did you get up on the wrong side of Nick's bed?"

In the past if Michelle had argued with Brooke, sometimes the asthma grew worse. Sometimes their feuding had brought on an attack, according to their mother. Michelle had learned long ago not to upset Brooke.

For those reasons Michelle didn't understand why at this point in time the emotional floodgates opened, but they did. Maybe it was all the pent-up concern struggling to come out. Her fear for Brooke and the baby. Nevertheless, she couldn't seem to stop saying what was on her mind. "I'll tell you what's wrong with me, Brooke Granger. I get so tired of your apathy when it comes to your asthma. Do you ever stop to think how much worry your asthma has caused? How much worry it's still causing now that you're going to have a baby?"

"You sound just like Mom. Of course I know. My asthma hasn't made me stupid."

"I know that, but sometimes I wonder. I've always wondered...all those years I wished..."

"Wished what, Michelle?"

"Never mind."

"You finish, dammit. You say what's on your mind

because—'' she paused to draw a breath ''—I'm not hanging up until you do.''

Reality sank in, halting Michelle's tirade. What was she doing, unloading on Brooke like this? What on earth had she hoped to accomplish?

''It's not important, Brooke.''

''It's important to me.'' The sound of Brooke's inhaler broke in to the suddenly awkward silence. ''Admit it, Michelle. You resented me.''

''I did not!''

''You did, and you had every right to. Mom treated us differently. She always has. You had to be the good girl and I got away with murder. If you say you didn't realize that, then you're a liar.''

Michelle hated herself at the moment. Hated that Brooke had touched on some deep-seated feelings that Michelle had no business unearthing. ''Okay, yes, I admit it. But that's selfish on my part. You were sick, not me.''

''Michelle, you are the most unselfish person I know. You were always there for me, for everyone, as a matter of fact. It's that same selflessness that got you involved with that other damned doctor. Not once did you turn your back on someone when they needed you. Not once, and it's cost you.''

Michelle fought her own tears. ''You don't understand. At times I was there for you because I had to be, not because I wanted to be.''

''Are you saying you didn't love me?''

''No!'' Michelle lowered her voice. ''I loved you. I still do. But sometimes I resented you because you were sick, and that makes me so ashamed.''

Brooke took in a ragged breath. ''You don't think I didn't hate you sometimes, Michelle? You were a cheerleader. I was your basic bookworm. You don't think I didn't envy you? I envied the fact that all the guys were in love with you. Envied your damned healthy lungs. And speaking of that, let's get to the bottom of this.''

''What do you mean?''

''You feel guilty because you're the healthy child. That's it, isn't it? If you could, you'd take my place without a second thought.''

Michelle pondered that concept for a moment. Was that it? Did she feel bad because she was the ''healthy'' one? It didn't matter now. The only thing that mattered was making it up to Brooke somehow.

''I'm so sorry, Brooke. I should never have upset you like this.''

''I'm okay, Michelle.'' She coughed again, harder this time. ''I need to go. I'm not feeling so great at the moment.'' She sounded even worse to Michelle.

''Brooke, I hope I didn't cause—''

''You didn't cause anything, Shelly.'' She drew in a halting, labored breath. ''You don't have that much power over me. Unfortunately, sometimes this asthma does. I'll talk to you when you get home.''

The line went dead then, and a part of Michelle died, too. She tossed the phone aside and stared at it for a few moments. How could she be so insensitive as to upset Brooke like that? How could she be such a careless fool?

Lowering her head into the cradle of her hands, Michelle cried. Cried over the fact she might have done irreparable damage to their relationship and contributed to Brooke's distress. Cried because she felt so unworthy of the happiness she had felt in Nick's arms. Cried because deep down, she knew she was falling in love with Nick Kempner, and that scared her almost as much as upsetting Brooke.

"It's okay, babe."

Nick's strong arms enfolded her against his solid chest. He tucked her head beneath his chin while she sobbed uncontrollably. She relished his comfort but in turn felt unworthy of his solace. Still, she clung to him until the tears began to subside, helpless to move away from him, knowing she probably should.

Staring into his understanding brown eyes, she muttered a lame apology.

He kissed her face, her lips, and said, "You don't need to be sorry. But you do need to talk to me."

"I don't know…if I can." Her words drifted off on a lingering sob. "I need to go home. I need to check on Brooke."

"Brooke's got Jared to take care of her. You need to come back to bed and let me take care of you, at least for a while."

She sniffed. "I'm fine. Really."

He stroked his knuckles over her damp jaw. "I won't take no for an answer. And I'll be there to listen when you're ready to talk, or we can just hold each other. Whatever you want." Standing, he pulled her to her feet. "I'll grab some coffee and be back up in a minute. In the meantime, go wash your face and wait for me."

"I don't know—"

He touched a fingertip to her lips. "All you need to know right now is that I'm here for you. We'll deal with the rest as we go. Promise you won't run out on me?"

She nodded her head and he dropped his finger from

her lips to replace it with his own lips. "Great. Yell if you need anything else."

Right now Michelle needed Nick, only Nick, and that scared her almost as much as having to face Brooke when she returned home. "Okay."

Nick headed to the kitchen, and Michelle headed back to bed. She dropped the phone onto the charger and propped herself up against the headboard, clutching a pillow to her chest. She felt exhausted, emotionally drained, guilty. How could such a wonderful weekend turn out so badly?

If she chose to stay, they still had tomorrow before she would be forced to face the consequences of the phone call. Maybe Nick could help her forget, at least for a little longer.

He joined her a few moments later carrying a tray that held two cups of coffee. After setting the tray on the nightstand, he slipped into bed beside her and yanked the pillow from her grasp, then drew her close to his side.

"How much did you hear?" she asked, although she wasn't certain she wanted to know.

"Enough to realize what's going on with you."

"I'm surprised you haven't sent me packing."

"Hey." He tipped her chin up and forced her to look at him. "You might not be an angel, Michelle, but you're not a horrible person. Not even close."

"That's what you think."

"That's what I know." He scooted around to face her with legs crossed and took her hand into his. "I realized a while back that you've suffered because of Brooke's asthma. I knew it that day I found you crying in the kitchen after Brooke announced her pregnancy."

Michelle swiped her eyes with the back of her free hand. "Definitely not one of my finer moments."

"You had every right to be upset. Brooke should have told you about the baby, and your concerns for her health are valid. Stop beating yourself up because you're human."

She released an inelegant snort. "Human? I had no cause to upset Brooke like I did."

"What about all those times you were upset? All those times your life was put on hold because of Brooke's illness? Did you talk to anyone about it?"

Obviously, Nick had heard more of the conversation than she'd realized. "I dealt with it. Brooke was the one who suffered, not me."

"You're wrong, Michelle. You did suffer. You're still suffering, and I hate like hell to see you this way. And I hate even worse the fact that some jerk took advantage of your generosity and you think that's what I'll do, too. You didn't deserve what he did to you and I'm not like him. I don't expect you to be perfect."

"Good. I'm not."

"You say you aren't, but you still put unreasonable demands on yourself. You don't think you have any right to consider what you need."

"I need to go back to bed and forget this ever happened."

Nick's sigh came out rough, frustrated. "You need to face the truth. You're a beautiful, compassionate woman, but you don't give yourself enough credit."

His words were a soothing balm for her soul, but reality kept rearing its ugly head. "I'm a failure at relationships, Nick. I've never been good at letting down my guard. When I have, I always seem to get hurt or hurt someone in the process."

His smile was gentle. "You're doing it now. You're letting me in."

"That's because you're making me do it."

Nick studied her as if he could see right through her. "Have you ever considered that maybe you've set yourself up to fail because you don't think you deserve to be loved?"

"Maybe I don't."

"You're wrong."

She sighed. "Am I? Look what I just did to Brooke. She probably hates me now, and I don't blame her."

"She doesn't hate you, and neither do I."

Michelle felt the urge again to protect her emotions, give Nick the out he needed. "Now that you know all my secrets, you don't have to hang around."

He dropped her hand and laced his hands behind his neck. "Dammit, Michelle, you're doing it again. Do you think that your presumed faults would make me love you any less?"

Had she heard right? Did he really say "love"? Her lips parted to speak, but nothing came out, any response blocked by a mammoth lump in her throat.

He caught both her hands and brought them to his lips for a gentle kiss. "That's right, Michelle. I said I love you. It might not make much sense, but it's the truth. And you know something? I think I fell in love with you that day at Jared and Brooke's wedding, right in front of the ice sculpture."

Michelle laughed through residual tears. "But I insulted you."

"And I was hitting on you."

"True, you were."

"Since that day," he said, "I've come to see a lot of great things about you. You're good with kids, my kid. You have a wicked sense of humor. You think about everyone but yourself, and that's admirable. To a point. But the thing I love most about you is the way that I feel when I'm around you. The way you make me feel, glad to be alive beyond my work as a doctor. I appreciate that more than you can know, and I don't intend to let a good thing get away.''

Nick's wonderful words spun around Michelle's brain like an out-of-control carousel. Nick loved *her*, Michelle Lewis, with all the fears and insecurities. What had she done to deserve his love, especially now?

''Nick, I—'' She couldn't stop the onslaught of tears or the fear of voicing her feelings.

He framed her face in his palms and wiped the moisture with his thumbs. ''Do you always cry when someone tells you they love you?''

''No one ever has before. At least not a man.''

He feathered a kiss across her cheek. ''Another thing I find hard to believe.''

Nick was making it difficult for her to regain some composure, but Michelle finally did with effort. ''It's true.''

''How do you feel about me?''

Her chance had come to tell him. A chance that might not come again. Michelle couldn't stop the sudden assault of emotions any more than she could stop her feelings for Nick.

''I think I love you, too,'' she said on a rush of fresh tears.

He looked as though she had handed him the brass ring. ''Do you have to sound so damned happy about it?''

''I'm not... I am... Oh, heck, I don't know. This is nuts.''

He kissed her then, a brief kiss brimming with tenderness. "No, Michelle, this is right. And however long it takes to convince you that you're a lovable person, I'm in there for the long haul."

Michelle desperately wanted to believe him, wanted so much to believe that she could have a future with Nick in spite of past failures. All she could do was cling to that hope.

He took her into his arms and laid her back on the bed. He simply held her in his strong embrace, whispering consolations, lulling her with soft kisses.

Michelle wasn't sure how long they had stayed that way, or how long they had been asleep when the phone rang once again.

Nick took one arm from around her and grabbed the phone next to where the coffee sat, untouched. "Yeah?"

After a few moments he released her and rose abruptly to the edge of the bed. "We'll be there as soon as we can."

As if in slow motion, Michelle sat up, panic pressing hard against her chest. "What's wrong?"

Nick turned to her, still clutching the phone, his expression etched with concern.

"Brooke's in labor."

Nothing Nick said convinced Michelle that it wasn't her fault. He tried to talk to her the first half of the return trip into town, yet she raised an intangible wall between them. He then opted to give her the silence she requested—not through words but through her actions when she turned away from him and stared out the window.

Driving over the speed limit, Nick made it to Memorial in record time. He parked in the doctors' lot and followed Michelle into the hospital, giving her space, giving her time. He hoped to God that he would somehow find a way to reach her, break through the emotional barrier she had erected.

They rode the elevator in silence to the labor and delivery floor. Once in the hallway, he stopped Michelle by taking her arm and turning her to face him before they reached the waiting room.

"Are you going to be okay?" he asked.

She nodded, but she didn't look at all okay. Her blue eyes, full of fear, of remorse, brimmed with unshed tears. Nick wanted to make it better, to kiss away her pain, but he knew she wouldn't accept his comfort now. Maybe not ever.

When they passed the nurses' station, Nick paused and asked, "Where's Brooke Granger?"

"In 512, Dr. Kempner, but the family's in the waiting area," one nurse offered.

"Has she delivered?"

"Not yet."

"That's good," Nick said to Michelle as they continued toward the waiting room. She didn't answer, only stared straight ahead as if she'd retreated into some world Nick wasn't allowed to enter.

Brooke and Michelle's parents stood in one corner of the small area talking quietly with Jared. When Nick guided Michelle toward them, she froze in her tracks.

Turning to Nick, she said, "I don't think I can face them," her voice high with panic.

"You have to, Michelle."

Her gaze jerked away. "They'll hate me for what I've done."

He gave her shoulders a little shake to draw her attention. "Look at me, Michelle." She did, slowly. "You haven't done anything. This isn't your fault."

"Yes, it is. I made her—"

"You didn't make her do anything, dammit. It would take more than an argument to send someone into labor."

"You didn't hear her, Nick. She was crying and I—"

"Oh, Shelly, I'm so glad you're here." Jeanie Lewis rushed over to them, arms outstretched.

Michelle hugged her mother with robotic movements. When she pulled back, she asked, "How is she?"

"Come over here and talk to Jared." Jeanie linked her arm through Michelle's and looked back at Nick over one shoulder. "Dr. Kempner, how nice of you to come and see about Brooke."

Obviously, Jeanie Lewis had no idea that Michelle had been with him for the past few days, and Nick had no intention of making her the wiser. "No problem, Mrs. Lewis."

He followed the pair into the middle of the waiting room and held out his hand to Jared, who looked like the backside of hell.

"Tell me what's happening, bud," Nick said.

Jared streaked a hand over his jaw. "They've given her meds to stop the labor and steroids to develop the baby's lungs, but a few minutes ago her water broke."

Michelle gasped. "So the baby's going to come today?"

"Looks that way," Jared said, his voice rough with emotion.

"And Brooke, is she okay?" Michelle asked.

Jared leaned back against the wall. "She's had a

rough time breathing, but she's doing okay right now. Her obstetrician was considering a C-section, but so far the baby's not showing any signs of distress and it looks like they'll let things progress naturally.''

"That's probably best," Nick said, recalling his brief rotation in OB, most of which he'd slept through. "The longer the baby waits to be delivered, the more steroids it will receive to strengthen its lungs.''

Jared turned his gaze to the ceiling. "Yeah, and with Brooke's asthma, I don't want them to put her out unless they have to." He paused a long moment. "If anything happens to her…''

Michelle stepped forward. "What are you saying, Jared?''

He drew in a slow breath. "There can be other babies, but I'll never find another Brooke.''

Nick felt as if he'd been gut punched. He could relate to Jared's anguish. Just the thought of something happening to Michelle or Kelsey constricted his chest from fear.

Jeanie Lewis sobbed, bringing Howard Lewis up behind her. He braced his hands on her shoulders. "It's going to be okay, honey. Brooke's a fighter. Everything's going to be okay.''

"Dr. Granger, your wife needs you," a nurse called from down the hall.

Jared spun around and headed down the corridor calling, "I'll let you know what's going on.''

Michelle sank into a nearby chair and hugged her arms to her chest. "This is all my fault. All my fault.''

The declaration drew Jeanie's attention from her husband's consolation, exactly what Nick had feared. "What are you talking about, Shelly?''

''We argued,'' Michelle said. ''This morning. I upset her, and now she's paying for it.''

Jeanie's eyes widened with shock. ''Good Lord, Michelle, what were you thinking? Don't you remember how many times Brooke's asthma was brought on by stress?''

''Yes, I remember.'' Michelle rocked back and forth. ''I wasn't thinking.''

Nick hated seeing Michelle beating herself up. ''As I told Michelle earlier, Mrs. Lewis, Brooke's early labor probably had nothing to do with the argument. Maybe not even the asthma.'' He crouched beside Michelle and stared at her straight on. ''I'm not going to let you do this to yourself. You've got to hang in there for Brooke.''

''Dr. Kempner's right,'' Jeanie said. ''You've inherited all the strength, enough for Brooke. Enough for all of us. You've always been the strong one. You can't fall apart on me now.''

''You're wrong, Mom,'' Michelle said, her voice thick with anger. ''I'm not strong at all. You just expected me to be.''

Nick recognized Michelle was right. Beneath that strong veneer lay a frightened little girl, one that had probably taken the blame for many things, and still blamed herself for her presumed shortcomings. Her mother had obviously contributed to that attitude by her unreasonable expectations and overprotective behavior when it came to Brooke.

After sending Jeanie a cautioning look, Howard walked to Michelle and placed a hand on the top of her lowered head. ''You're going to be fine, Shelly girl. If it makes you feel better, then go ahead and cry. But just remember, it's all going to be okay. I can feel it in my gut.''

Michelle looked up and sent him a weak smile. "Thanks, Daddy.''

Jared suddenly reappeared. "The baby's coming. Michelle, Brooke wants you with us.''

Michelle looked terrified. "Me?''

"There must be some mistake," Jeanie said, wringing her hands. "I'm her mother. I'm sure Brooke wants me there.''

"No mistake," Jared said.

"But—''

"She wants Michelle with her, Jeanie.'' Jared looked as though his composure was about ready to snap. Understandable, Nick thought, since his own impatience with Michelle's mother had reached immense proportions. But this wasn't his battle, so he would leave it up to Jared to set the woman straight.

Jared gave Jeanie a stern look. "We'll have a whole team in there, so there's only room for one more, and Brooke asked for Michelle. We have to honor that request, and I don't have time to argue.''

Stepping back, Jeanie dabbed at her eyes with a crinkled tissue. "Okay, if that's what she wants, then I'll just sit out here and wait by myself.''

Howard Lewis ran a hand over his scalp and released a frustrated sigh. "Good grief, woman! What am I, chopped liver?'' He gestured toward the hall. "You two go on. Just have someone let us know what's happening when you can.''

Michelle stood, her spine stiff. "Let Mom go in. I don't think I can do it.''

Taking Michelle by the shoulders once again, Nick

said, "You have to do this. Brooke needs you. You've always been there for her. Don't give up now."

She studied him a long moment before raising her chin in determination. "You're right. I can do this."

Eleven

Michelle couldn't do this, not with Brooke propped up in the bed with an oxygen mask over her mouth, her face contorted with pain. But Michelle had to do it, for Brooke's sake, although for the life of her, she didn't understand why her sister wanted her there.

Moving around the chaos of medical staff readying for the birth, Michelle stood next to Jared.

Brooke slipped the mask down and said, "Hi, Shelly. I'm glad you're here."

Michelle took the hand she offered. "Me, too. I think. Does it hurt much?"

"Like a son of a—oh, here it goes again. I have to push."

"Okay, Brooke," the doctor said from her place at the end of the bed. "Let's get this baby born."

Michelle stepped back from the bed and allowed Jared to position Brooke for the final stage of labor.

He encouraged her sister with firm but gentle commands; Brooke responded by never taking her eyes from his.

Michelle watched in awe as Brooke and Jared worked together to bring their child into the world. She found herself mentally counting to ten along with Brooke, Jared and the attending nurse. She felt Brooke's pain almost as keenly as if it were her own, just as she had so many times when they'd been kids and Brooke had been sick.

After the contraction, the doctor told Brooke to relax for a few moments.

The door opened to a tall, handsome man with shocking-green eyes and dark hair. He walked in dressed in scrubs like the rest of the staff, but Michelle didn't recognize him.

"Okay, I'm here," he said with a grin. "You can go ahead now, Brooke."

Brooke's brows drew down into a frown, and she tipped the mask up once again. "Thanks for your permission, Dr. O'Connor, and don't I wish." She glanced at Michelle. "Don't you want to take over for me now, Shelly? You were always better with pain."

If only Brooke realized how much Michelle wished she could take away the pain, all of it. But Michelle had never been able to do that. All she could offer was support. "You're doing great, Brooke. Just great."

Jared exchanged greetings with the mystery doctor, who then nodded at Michelle. "You must be Brooke's sister. I'm Brendan O'Connor, the neonatologist who'll be taking care of the baby. I'd shake your hand," he raised one gloved appendage, "but I can't at the moment."

"I understand," Michelle said. "It's nice to meet

you, too, but I wish it were under different circumstances."

"True, but rest assured I'll take good care of your niece or nephew."

"I'm counting on it," she muttered.

A long moan escaped Brooke's lips, signaling another contraction. More prodding from the doctor for Brooke to push and more words of encouragement from Jared echoed in the room. A nurse rolled in a portable incubator. The doctor announced the baby was almost there and requested that Brooke give one more small push.

Michelle looked up in the overhead mirror and saw the moment the baby thrust its way into the world.

"It's a boy," the doctor declared.

A boy. Brooke and Jared had a son. Michelle had a nephew. A tiny boy no bigger than the doctor's hands.

Nothing but silence followed. No cry of protest. Nothing.

Jared and Brooke, caught up in an embrace, exchanged a fearful look. A flurry of activity immediately followed the cord being cut. A nurse handed the baby to Dr. O'Connor, who began to issue orders in an even tone. Something about "bagging the baby" some kind of scores, a "vent," but still the baby didn't cry.

But Brooke did, and so did Michelle when her sister pleaded to hold her son and was immediately but gently denied that privilege. Jared tried to comfort Brooke, but he looked as though he might be on the verge of tears himself.

Dr. O'Connor assured them all that the baby was alive but struggling. A little over three pounds, with underdeveloped lungs, but alive—and fighting.

The room began to close in on Michelle. She could

no longer endure the fear that was almost palpable, or Brooke's distress, or watching the baby boy born too soon struggle to survive. It was all too much.

Unable to endure the atmosphere, Michelle slipped from the room without much notice. No one questioned her. No one asked where she was going. Why should anyone care? She felt a stifling guilt that maybe this *was* her fault, and if the baby didn't make it, she might never be able to live down the guilt.

She found Nick in the corridor, one shoulder cocked against the wall, his arms crossed over his chest.

He pushed off the wall as soon as Michelle passed him heading away from the waiting area.

"Michelle, stop."

She didn't, not until she turned the corner and found herself in a small alcove, a dead-end thankfully void of people. Tipping her head against the rough-textured enclosure, she tried to cry some more, but the tears wouldn't come, at least not at the moment. Guilt was her only companion now—and Nick who had caught up with her.

He enfolded her in his arms from behind and rested his forehead against the back of her head. "The baby?"

"A boy," she said dryly.

"Is he okay?"

"He's not breathing on his own, that's all I know."

Nick turned her around but didn't let her go. "That's normal. He's premature. They'll put him on a ventilator to help him breathe and do several tests. Standard procedure."

"Maybe for you, Nick, but not for me. That's Brooke and Jared's baby, not just some anonymous patient."

Anger flashed in his dark eyes as he released her. "Don't you think I know that? Don't you think I hurt like hell for them? Jared's my best friend, and I know how I would've felt if anything had happened to Kelsey."

"I'm sorry. Of course you know." Michelle felt shamed and worn out. She needed to get out of there, be alone, try to think, and to pray. "Can you take me home now?"

His features softened. "You don't want to stay a little longer and see—"

"If he dies?"

"If Brooke needs you."

"As you said, Brooke has Jared now."

"And you have me."

But she didn't deserve him. Feeling liquid-boned, she leaned against the wall. "I need some time, Nick. I need to be by myself."

He braced one hand above her head and nailed her with a stern glare. "So you can wallow in self-pity?"

That hurt almost as much as the prospect of letting him go. But right now she had to let him go. "This doesn't have anything to do with you and me. This has to do with my family."

"And I guess that doesn't include me, does it?" He straightened, pain flashing in his dark eyes. "Fine. I'll take you home, but I'm not going away."

The trip to Michelle's apartment was a repeat of the trip back from the lake house. Michelle sat in silence, staring out the window, while Nick tried to plan what he needed to say. She was hurting, that much he knew. But he hurt, too, knowing she was shutting him out.

Maybe only temporarily, but that didn't make the ache in his heart go away.

They'd both admitted their love for each other that morning, great moments that now seemed ages ago. Had he been too quick in his admission to her? Had she reconsidered her feelings for him? Should he ask her that now, or give her more time to think?

When they pulled into the space closest to Michelle's apartment, Nick cut off the engine and geared up to have a long talk. Michelle had other ideas. She hurriedly slid out of the car without even so much as a goodbye. Distressed and determined, Nick followed her up the stairs and stopped her before she could get her key into the door.

"Can I come in?" he asked.

She reluctantly faced him and sighed. "I told you, I need to be alone."

"I don't think you do."

"What you think doesn't matter."

"Well, thanks, Michelle. I'm glad to know it. I'm glad I wasted my breath telling you how I feel about you only to have you slam the door in my face, literally."

She turned the key over and over in her hand but failed to look at him. "I'm sorry for everything. Maybe this weekend was a mistake."

"It wasn't a mistake, Michelle. The only mistake is you shutting me out. When two people love each other, they're supposed to lean on each other." He brushed her hair away from her shoulders. "And I do love you."

She finally raised her eyes to his. "I'm sorry for that, too. You can do a lot better than me."

"Why don't you let me be the judge of that?"

"I need to go, Nick. I don't feel like talking right now."

Realizing that her stress was doing the talking, he lowered his voice. "Okay, you take some time alone. But if you need me, even if it's just to talk, call me."

"I don't need to talk, Nick. I don't need anything, or anyone. Not now."

He walked a fine line between anger and hurt, between shaking some sense into her and kissing her pain away. "Okay, that's great, so you don't need anyone. But your fear is in danger of destroying something really good between us. Something real that we both deserve. And don't worry about talking, but you damn sure better listen, because I'm only going to say this once."

Drawing in a deep breath, he continued, even knowing that his temper had overcome his common sense. "I'm not like your mother, Michelle. I don't expect you to be strong all the time, and I won't give up on you during your moments of weakness. And I'm not like your married lover. I haven't lied to you about anything and I don't take commitment lightly. I never have—in my work, even in my marriage. I fought for both because I believe that's what you do if you want to make something work. I've been fighting for you, for us."

He paused for a long moment, preparing for the hardest thing he had to say to her. "But I've also learned when to back off and when to call it quits. So the rest is up to you, Michelle. If you want to make this work between us, then you'll have to come to me. I'm not going to beg you. And until you decide what you do want, I won't bother you again."

With that, he headed away. Left before he took her

in his arms and tried to convince her the best way he knew how, with a kiss, with lovemaking that would make them both forget. But he wouldn't fall into old patterns. Sex served as little more than putting a small bandage on a giant wound. It wasn't enough to make things all better, especially not this time.

So he chose to walk away, get in his car and drive off. Walk away from the woman he loved with his heart and soul, because he refused to make the same mistakes again. If she didn't want his consolation, fine. If she refused to believe that he cared about her more than he had ever cared for any woman, fine. If she didn't want him, fine. He could live without her, even if he didn't want to.

God, he didn't want to.

On Monday morning Michelle drove to the hospital an hour early and stayed in the parking lot for endless moments to convene her courage.

She had sat alone all day Sunday thinking about Brooke, about her new nephew and about Nick.

Michelle had called the hospital several times to check on Brooke and the baby, discovering that her nephew had been listed as stable. Brooke had been in good condition and resting with a request for no visitors. Michelle had chosen not to return her mother's phone calls until she'd had more time to regroup. Twice she had picked up the phone to call Nick. Twice she had hung up before the phone rang.

After mulling over the situation for the better part of twenty-four hours, she'd come to the decision to see Brooke this morning and set things straight. She'd come to no decisions about her relationship with Nick. She loved him; she couldn't deny that. Her feelings had become more apparent after their weekend together and then spending last night without him in her arms. She longed to be with him, yet she feared taking that step. He had been right about her wallowing in self-pity. She needed to put a halt to those feelings. Talking to Brooke was the first step on her journey to snap out of it.

After making her way to Brooke's room, Michelle gently rapped on the door. Brooke called for her to come in. Michelle walked quietly inside, prepared to beg for forgiveness.

Jared sat at the bedside, the room filled with every flower imaginable, all shapes and sizes arranged in an assortment of vases. When Brooke met Michelle's gaze, she smiled. "Well look what the cat dragged in. My long-lost sister."

Michelle took a tentative step forward. "Is it a good time? I mean, if you need to rest—"

"Of course it's a good time, silly."

Jared stood and cleared his throat. "I'll leave you two girls with it. I'll go check on the baby and then I'll be at the office for a while."

"Matthew," Brooke corrected. "We can't keep calling him 'the baby.'"

Jared gave her a sad smile. "Yeah, you're right." He bent and kissed Brooke. "I'll see you at lunch. I love you."

"I love you, too," Brooke said.

Michelle's heart sank, not from envy but from the fact that she could possibly experience this same bond with Nick. But after what she had said to him the last time they'd been together, she doubted that would happen.

When Jared brushed past Michelle and walked out

the door, Brooke nodded toward the chair in the corner. "Sit a spell."

"I don't have too long," Michelle said, making her way to the chair. "I have to play catch-up today."

Once she had settled in, Brooke eyed her for a long moment. "I recognize that hangdog look on your face, Shelly. And I have a feeling I know why."

Michelle's guilt caused her to look away. "I'm sorry, Brooke. For everything. This whole thing is all my fault."

"Stop right there. This was not your fault. It was my fault."

Michelle's gaze snapped back to Brooke. "How can you say that? You have no control over your asthma."

"It wasn't the asthma or our conversation that caused the early labor."

"How do you know?"

Brooke folded and unfolded the sheet's edge. "Because I fell, that's how I know."

Michelle's mouth gaped open. "You fell?"

"Yeah. You know I've never been as graceful as you. I was on a step stool cleaning when the stool tipped and I did a nice dive onto the kitchen floor."

"What were you doing on a step stool?"

"Dusting. Mom and Dad were coming for dinner."

Michelle held up a hand. "Say no more."

They shared a laugh then, some of the burden lifting from Michelle.

Brooke laid her head back against the pillow. "So it was that and the combination of the asthma from stirring up the dust, not our minor argument."

"It wasn't a minor argument, Brooke. I was tough on you. I wish I could take back all the things I said."

"I'm glad you said them, and I'm glad that we now

have it all out in the open." Brooke studied the ceiling for a moment. "You know, we've always been two peas in a pod. You've always been my hero. You still are. That doesn't mean you don't make me mad now and then, but there's nothing, *nothing* you could ever do that would be beyond my forgiveness, and I hope that holds true for you."

Michelle's eyes misted. She rose and took Brooke's hand. "Yes, that's true. And for the record, you're my hero, too."

They hugged each other hard as they had so many times before. When Michelle straightened, she asked, "How's the ba—" She smiled. "How's Matthew?"

"Doing much better than expected. Dr. O'Connor is very optimistic. He has no reason to believe that Matthew won't make it. He says my son is a fighter and has the tenacity of a pit bull."

"Wonder where he gets that."

"From you and me, I imagine. And, of course, his doctor father. On that note, there's something I want to ask you."

"Shoot."

"What's going on with you and Nick?"

Michelle wasn't in the proper frame of mind to discuss Nick. Just hearing his name caused an ache that branched out from her heart to settle soul deep. "I haven't seen him since Saturday."

"I know. Jared says he's a wreck, moping around like a little lost puppy. So what's going on?"

Covering her face with her hands, Michelle proclaimed, "I blew it."

Brooke yanked Michelle's hands down. "What do you mean you blew it?"

"I told him I didn't need anything, or anyone. But the truth is, I need him."

"But do you love him?"

Michelle sighed. "Yes, with everything in me."

"Okay, dummy, then what are you doing here?"

"Visiting you."

Brooke slapped her hand on the rolling tray-table next to the bed, startling Michelle. "Visit's over. Get your butt in gear and go find Nick."

Oh, how Michelle wanted to do that. How she wanted to tell him everything in her heart and try to make things right. But was it too late for that? "He probably doesn't want to see me."

"You'll never know until you try, will you? Lord knows you're not one to let something you want pass you by. So find him and tell him how you feel."

Nick's words came back to Michelle, sharp as shards of glass, cutting her heart to the quick.

Until you decide what you do want, I won't bother you again.

In that moment Michelle knew exactly what she wanted—Nick. She wanted to spend her days with him, her nights, her life. Maybe he had reconsidered, but as Brooke had said, Michelle wouldn't know unless she tried. She had never hesitated when going after a goal, and that included her goal to have Nick make love with her at the lake house. Little had she known her dog-gedness would have led to love. Could that determination save her from a life without Nick? Might as well find out.

Grinning, Michelle gave Brooke another hug. "You're absolutely right, Brookie. I'm going to find him and make him let me grovel."

"Good plan, Michelle."

"I'll do it tonight."

"Do it now, before any more time passes. We've both learned that's the best way to handle everything."

"But I don't know where he is."

"At his office until noon. He came by during rounds and mentioned he'd be there if we needed him."

Good to know, since Michelle needed him more than anything she had ever needed in her life. "Should I go to his office now? Just show up unannounced?"

"Why not?"

She could think of several reasons why it might not be such a great idea, the first being she didn't like the thought of getting booted out on her butt. But as they said, nothing ventured, nothing gained.

Taking a resolute breath, Michelle nodded. "Okay. I'll go to his office and spill my guts."

Brooke pointed to a vase on the shelf. "Take him some flowers. I've got plenty. It can't hurt."

"You know, you're right."

Michelle whisked one vase full of yellow roses from the shelf and gave Brooke a parting hug along with a promise to fill her in on the details that afternoon.

She silently made her way to the lower level and the hallway leading to the adjoining medical complex. Once in the lobby she searched the board and found Nick's suite number. Seeing his name brought on out-and-out excitement, along with another spear of apprehension. What if he really did refuse to hear her out? She had come this far, no use turning back now.

Once she reached Nick's office, Michelle stepped inside the reception area and made her way to the sliding glass window, her palms perspiring where they circled the vase.

The receptionist looked up and smiled. "May I help you?"

"I need to see Nick—Dr. Kempner."

The woman surveyed the flowers with curiosity. "I can give those to him for you."

"I have to deliver them personally."

"But—"

"Please. I'm his friend." Or so she hoped.

"Okay, I can ask him, but he's got office hours this morning."

"This won't take long." Maybe not more than a minute, Michelle thought, if Nick decided that he wanted nothing more to do with her.

"Your name?"

"Michelle."

"Last name?"

"He'll know who I am." Unless he had already made a conscious effort to forget her.

"I'll be right back."

The lady returned after a few minutes and directed Michelle through the door from the waiting room. Michelle walked the hall with head held high although she felt lower than a slug. She supposed that's what groveling should entail, belly-crawling. In her peripheral vision she noted several of the staff staring as she headed toward his office.

Arriving at the end of the corridor, she found the door open and Nick kicked back in his chair, hands behind his neck, feet propped on the edge of the desk. A gorgeous, dark, imposing backdrop to the morning sun shining through the windows behind him. But he wasn't smiling.

Michelle slipped inside, clutching the flowers against her chest like a life preserver. All coherent greetings lodged in her throat when he pinned her with his midnight eyes.

"Close the door," he said, his voice a low command.

Michelle complied then leaned back against it.

"Peace offering?" he asked, his tone bordering on sarcasm.

"Something like that," she replied, thankful her voice had come back to her. Now if only her brain would make an appearance.

"To what do I owe this unexpected visit?"

She pushed off the door. "You told me that when I made my decision, I needed to come to you. So here I am."

He dropped his feet from the desk and leaned forward, hands clasped before him. "And what did you decide?"

"That I love you and I miss you and I need you." Nothing like getting straight to the point, Michelle thought.

Nick slowly stood, came around the desk and leaned back against it, arms crossed over his chest, his dark gaze leveled on her. "Are you sure about that?"

"As sure as I've ever been in my life."

He scrubbed a hand over his clean-shaven jaw and looked beyond her. He didn't speak, but his expression spoke volumes. She could tell he wasn't certain how to respond. She couldn't blame him. She also couldn't stand his silence a minute longer.

"Say something, Nick. Tell me to get lost, get out of your life. Tell me I'm a fool, I screwed up, anything, but please put me out of my misery."

"I'm thinking," he finally said.

Michelle stomped her foot, a stupid childish thing to

do, but she did it, anyway, regardless of her vow to remain composed. "I know that, but *what* are you thinking?"

"I'm thinking I wish you would just shut up and kiss me."

The words rang in her ears. "What?"

"You heard me."

He strolled toward her, hands hidden in the pockets of his lab coat. "I'm also thinking that you have put me through the worst kind of hell over the past two days. I'm thinking that I'm crazy—about you. I'm thinking that I can't believe you're here, telling me you need me."

Michelle's heart flip-flopped in her chest. "I am, and I do. I meant everything I said. All of it."

He stood toe-to-toe with her this time, bringing with him a mist of heady cologne that brought Michelle's senses to life. But he didn't touch her no matter how badly she wanted him to. "Before I do kiss you, or take you back, there's one condition."

Her heart dropped to her shoes. "What condition?"

"You say yes."

Here we go again. "To what?"

"To marrying me."

She never would have believed that those two words could send her mind into a total tailspin. Then again, she'd never thought to hear them, at least from Nick. "Marry you?"

"Yeah, if that's not just a totally repulsive idea. That's what people who love each other do. They make a commitment. And I figure that's the only way I'm going to keep you from running like the wind if things don't always go smoothly."

"But... I..." Why was she stammering like an idiot? The man had proposed to her. A good man. Correction. A great man. A gorgeous, sensual doctor. A wonderful, caring father. A man who loved her.

He reached out and touched her face. "What's the matter? Cat got your tongue?"

Obviously. One with big claws. "I'm thinking." Thinking she was nuts for even considering such a thing. Thinking she would be even nuttier if she didn't say yes.

She loved him more than she could say. She couldn't imagine not spending the rest of her days with him. And he loved her, even after the heartache she'd put him through. Even after he'd seen the real Michelle, faults and all. More important, he wanted to *marry* her.

"Yes." My gosh, she did it! And lightning didn't strike, but the earth did move beneath her feet. She felt buoyed, light-headed, delirious.

"Okay, then," he said with no more than a satisfied smile.

Okay, then? She hadn't expected that. But when did Nick ever do anything she'd expected? The best part of his charm.

He didn't take her in his arms or kiss her. Instead he walked behind her toward the door, away from her. Was that it? *Okay, we'll get married, I'm going to work now?*

Immobilized by her shock, Michelle stood in the same spot and stared at the desk. But she didn't hear the door open. She did hear the lock trip. Maybe he wasn't going back to work after all. That brought about a strong case of gooseflesh spreading all over Michelle's body over the prospect of what Nick might be planning.

He brushed past her again and headed to his desk

while Michelle waited for what would come next. Pressing the phone's intercom, he said, "Marlene, hold all my calls, no visitors, no interruptions."

"But Dr. Kempner, you have patients in fifteen minutes," the receptionist replied.

Nick grinned at Michelle. "Fifteen minutes is all I need, *if* you leave me alone."

"Yes, Doctor."

He then cut off the intercom, methodically took off his lab coat, hung it on the coat tree in the corner, yanked off his tie and belt to join the lab coat, while Michelle continued to stand in the same spot, speechless, gripping the vase of roses. Slipping the buttons on his blue shirt, he sauntered toward her.

Michelle's pulse thrummed in time to her pounding heart when his tanned chest, sprinkled with just the right amount of nonobtrusive hair and well-defined muscle, came into view.

Tugging the vase from her grasp, Nick flipped up the card pinned to the blue ribbon. "Congratulations, Brooke and Jared. Love, Aunt June and Uncle Harry?"

"I had to improvise."

His grin deepened. "I guess it's the thought that counts. So this means you've seen your sister?"

"Yes."

"She told you about her fall?"

"Yes."

He turned and set the flowers on his desk, then came back to her. "Everything okay now?"

"Right as rain."

"Great." He worked his hands underneath the shoulders of Michelle's blazer, removed it slowly and tossed it onto the arm of the sofa behind her. "I suppose this isn't a good time to tell you 'I told you so.'"

Right now he could tell her anything he wanted and she'd agree. "I admit you were right."

"I've been right about a few things, but mainly I've been right about you. You're a good person, Michelle. You deserve the best in life."

For once she accepted that she was going to have the best—Nick Kempner, to be exact, starting now.

Reaching behind her, he unclasped her slacks and let them fall to the floor. Michelle braced her hands on his shoulders, kicked off her pants and stepped out of her shoes.

"I'm glad you said yes," he told her as he worked the buttons on her blouse. "Otherwise I couldn't have done this."

She drew in a sharp breath when he paused to place a wet kiss between her breasts. "Aren't you worried that the help will wonder what we're doing in here?" she asked, although she wasn't. In fact, she didn't care if a whole army of patients walked in, as long as Nick didn't stop.

Having completely unbuttoned her blouse, he took it off, pitched it onto the couch near her jacket and did the same with his shirt. Now Michelle was dressed only in pantyhose and bra. Nick wore only his slacks and a smile.

"You know something, babe?" He brought her against him and rimmed the shell of her ear with his tongue, sending pleasant chills spiraling down her spine. "I imagine I've been accused of doing this very thing at least a dozen times. I never have, but I might as well if everyone's intent on believing it."

He unclasped her bra and snapped it backward over his shoulder like a slingshot. It landed on top of his desk. "Are you all for starting some rumors?"

She tracked his zipper down, proving she was more than ready to play along. "Let the rumors begin."

Nick backed her to the sofa and laid her down then relieved them of what little clothes remained. He kissed her deeply, a kiss full of emotion, of mutual need. He touched her with reverence, with grace, murmuring his love. She touched him back with awe, with hunger, knowing in that moment that this was truly where she belonged, in Nick's arms, making love so sweet it called up a few latent tears of joy.

With skilled fingertips, with his warm, masterful mouth, Nick took her to the limit in less time than it took to undress. Michelle welcomed his strength when he slipped inside her body and set a slow cadence that robbed her of breath, relieved her of all thought beyond the here and now. Together they loved as if nothing else mattered. Nothing else did, as far as Michelle was concerned.

When they were breathless and spent, clinging to each other on the small sofa as if it were a comfortable bed, Michelle braced her hands on his jaw and lifted his head from her shoulder to study his near-black eyes, his beautiful face. A face she would wake up to, go to bed to, from this point forward.

"Now that I've given you the goods, you are still going to marry me, aren't you?" she asked in a teasing tone.

He frowned. "Hmm. Let me think on that one."

"You'd better. If I lose my job because I'm late, you'll have to support me."

His expression turned serious. "I'll support you however you need me to. In your work, with your family, whatever it takes to make you happy."

"You know you're inheriting my mother, don't you?"

"Getting you in the deal will make it all worthwhile."

"Do you think we might take another fifteen minutes to practice for the honeymoon?"

Brushing her hair back from her face, he kissed her once again and gave her his charming smile. "We can take as long as you like, Michelle. Let everyone else wait. I've waited long enough for you."

Michelle couldn't agree more, but Dr. Nick Kempner had definitely been worth the wait.

Epilogue

Nick couldn't wait to get out of there.

The room was noisy and crowded, filled with family and friends—Jared and Brooke as attendants, Kelsey, who'd served as an enthusiastic flower girl, Nick and Michelle's parents along with Nick's three sisters as well as Cassandra Allen and various medical staff. They had all assembled in the hospital's private banquet room following the family-only wedding held in the first-floor chapel. A wedding that Nick and Michelle had managed to plan in six weeks' time.

With all the preparation and Michelle's need to wrap up the ad campaign, Nick's call schedule, the impromptu family get-togethers and last-minute wedding showers, they'd barely been alone. Most of the time Nick had communicated with Michelle by phone, conversations conducted between appointments or late at night from the hospital's E.R. They'd only made love twice since their office interlude, and Nick had suffered from the loss of quality time with Michelle, the lack of intimacy. He was still suffering, but at least now he could make up for that lost time, if they ever got on with the honeymoon.

Nick swiped the cake crumbs from his lapel when Michelle lovingly shoved a piece into his mouth after he licked the crumbs from her mouth while her family looked on. Oh, well. He no longer had to worry about his reputation now that she had made him an honest man. A man who honestly could think of little else than getting his beautiful wife alone and naked.

Drawing Michelle to his side, Nick kissed her cheek as the photographer continued to snap picture after picture, practically blinding him with the flash. "Let's get out of here, okay?"

"Great idea," she said through a fake smile. "These heels are killing me."

Nick took a long glance down Michelle's body encased in a sleeveless white satin dress that hugged her curves and set his body on fire as if someone had lit a torch below his cummerbund. "*You're* killing me," he muttered through clenched teeth. "Ten more minutes and I'm going to clear this table of that three-tiered cake and that champagne fountain and take you right here in front of all the guests."

She sent him a sideways glance. "You wouldn't dare."

He ran his hand up her back and tugged on the zipper at her neck. "Watch me."

Jared chose that exact moment to interrupt. "Are you guys about to leave?"

"If I had my way," Nick muttered.

Brooke joined her husband and slipped an arm around his waist. "If I were you, I'd hurry. Mom's heading this way. I think she's about to give Michelle a birds-and-bees talk."

"That's our cue to hit the road," Nick said. "The limo's waiting for us."

Michelle looked up at Nick with blue eyes still capable of bringing him to his knees. "Can we go see the baby first?"

He was in a big, big hurry at the moment to save his dignity, but he couldn't deny her that. He couldn't deny her anything, for that matter. "Okay. Lead the way."

"You two go on up," Brooke said. "We'll keep everyone occupied. Be sure to tell our son that Mommy and Daddy will see him in a bit." The couple headed off in the direction of Brooke's parents. Nick was more than thankful for the diversion.

"What about Kelsey?" Michelle asked, nodding toward Nick's daughter.

Nick glanced at Kelsey, holding her skirts high and dancing around like a sprite. "I've already told her goodbye. She's going to the hotel with my parents. They've promised her a day at the amusement park and lots of toys. She'll probably never miss me."

"I seriously doubt that," Michelle said. "In fact, I know she'll miss you. I would."

He hugged Michelle to him, grateful that she still considered everyone else's feelings, relieved that she had learned some moderation and had started to consider her own for a change. "We'll see her after we get back from Hawaii."

"I still can't believe we're going."

"Believe it, babe. Five days of water and sand. Lots of beach to explore." He brought his lips to her ear and whispered, "The perfect place to make love behind a palm tree."

She sent him a knowing smile. "Can I go topless?"

That did it. If Nick didn't get her out of here, he'd find the nearest supply closet.

Taking her hand, Nick rushed Michelle past the murmuring masses and entered a service elevator to the fifth floor. He stole a few kisses on the trip, along with a few touches that almost had him hitting the emergency stop button for a quickie. But he didn't want quick. He wanted all night. And soon.

Once they reached the NICU, they immediately ran into Brendan O'Connor coming out of the double doors.

"How's Matt?" Michelle asked.

"He's doing great. In fact, if all goes well, he should be going home the end of next week."

Michelle's expression lit up with pure joy. "Just in time for us to be back from the honeymoon. Thanks for getting him through this, Brendan. Can we see him for a minute?"

"Sure. Just grab a gown and go on in. I'll be back in a minute."

After entering the unit, they stood side by side at the scrub sink in the familiar hand-washing ritual. Afterward, Nick slipped the paper gown over his tux; Michelle did the same over her dress. He could only imagine how they looked to the staff members, considering all the stares they received—a couple of life-size fashion dolls invading the NICU.

Once they found Matt's crib, Nick pulled Michelle against him and wrapped his arms around her middle.

"Hey, you two. I thought you'd left."

Nick and Michelle looked simultaneously toward the doors at Brendan O'Connor and Cassandra Allen approaching side by side.

"Hi, Cassie," Michelle said. "I didn't know you two knew each other."

The pair stopped next to the crib. "We're good buddies," Cassie said, patting the neonatologist on the cheek.

Brendan grinned. "I let her win our tennis games."

Just friends. Yeah, right, Nick thought wryly when he noticed the way the doc looked at Cassie. More than friendship there. He'd bet his bonus on it.

Once the couple offered their congratulations and departed, Michelle leaned back against Nick. "He's beautiful, isn't he?"

"He's okay. A good doc, but I think your friend's already laid claim to him. Besides, you're a married woman."

"Not Dr. O'Connor, silly. My nephew."

"Good thing that's who you meant. I was getting a little jealous there."

She flashed him a dimple. "Do you really think something's going on with Cassie and Brendan?"

"I can recognize that look from a hundred paces. He's got it bad. He just doesn't know it yet."

Michelle sighed. "I hope so. I want everyone to be happy."

Nothing new there. Just one of the many reasons why Nick loved her so much. Exactly why he aimed to make her happy.

Nick turned his attention to Matthew Granger with his tiny hands drawn up in fists under his chin, like a flyweight boxer posed to deliver a punch. Appropriate. The boy was a champion fighter. "Yeah, this is a good-looking kid, all right, just like his aunt. Speaks well for prime genes."

Michelle looked back at him with undisguised love in her eyes. Nick couldn't remember ever feeling so damned satisfied.

"This is what it's all about, isn't it?" she said wistfully.

"You can say that again."

She rested her hand on Matt's crib. "Are we going to do this someday?"

"Sleep?"

She frowned. "Make a baby."

"How about tonight?"

"I said someday. Right now I don't want to share you. At least for a while."

Nick buried his face in her neck. "I don't want to share you, either, so tell your nephew goodbye for now."

Michelle reached into the crib and stroked the baby's cheek. "'Bye, little one. Sleep tight. I love you."

"And I love you," Nick found himself saying, not caring who heard the declaration.

She turned into his arms and looked at him as if he'd

handed her the key to heaven. "I love you, too." She planted a kiss on his chin. "And you'd better be ready, Dr. Kempner, because I plan on showing you just how much for the rest of my life."

He was more than ready—ready to start their life together, ready to prove to the world that he was a one-woman man, and that particular woman was standing right in front of him, loving him completely, both the good and the bad.

Today was only the beginning, and what a great beginning it was.

*   *   *   *   *

Don't miss the next book in
Kristi Gold's MARRYING AN M.D. *series.*

DR. DESTINY

will be out March 2002!

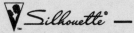

Silhouette® *Desire*

presents

DYNASTIES: THE CONNELLYS

A brand-new miniseries about the Connellys of Chicago,
a wealthy, powerful American family tied by blood to the
royal family of the island kingdom of Altaria.
They're wealthy, powerful and rocked by
scandal, betrayal…and passion!

Look for a whole year of glamorous and
utterly romantic tales in 2002:

January: **TALL, DARK & ROYAL by Leanne Banks**

February: **MATERNALLY YOURS by Kathie DeNosky**

March: **THE SHEIKH TAKES A BRIDE by Caroline Cross**

April: **THE SEAL'S SURRENDER by Maureen Child**

May: **PLAIN JANE & DOCTOR DAD by Kate Little**

June: **AND THE WINNER GETS…MARRIED! by Metsy Hingle**

July: **THE ROYAL & THE RUNAWAY BRIDE by Kathryn Jensen**

August: **HIS E-MAIL ORDER WIFE by Kristi Gold**

September: **THE SECRET BABY BOND by Cindy Gerard**

October: **CINDERELLA'S CONVENIENT HUSBAND
by Katherine Garbera**

November: **EXPECTING…AND IN DANGER by Eileen Wilks**

December: **CHEROKEE MARRIAGE DARE
by Sheri WhiteFeather**

Silhouette®
Where love comes alive™